TAKEN

ALANA WINTERS

Copyright © 2023 by Alana Winters

All rights reserved.

No part of this book may be reproduced in any form or by any electronic or mechanical means, including information storage and retrieval systems, without written permission from the author, except for the use of brief quotations in a book review.

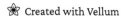 Created with Vellum

VANISHED IN BALTIMORE

I've always liked to play with fire. Now it's playing with me. Stella has kindled my dark heart, ignited my desires and set my world ablaze.

Before my life could even begin, it almost went up in flames.

Smoke alarms saved our lives.

The sound put my mother into labor.

The fire forged a powerful force in me.

I find resolve in its embers.

My enemies find their selves scorched by it.

It has never consumed me...not until I met its infernal match—Stella.

The red-hot firestorm that has me burning for more.

SOUNDTRACK

1) The Devil-BANKS
    2) Bad Blood-Taylor Swift
    3) Where Are You?-Elvis Drew, Avivian
    4) Whatever It Takes-Imagine Dragons
    5) Stellar-Incubus
    6) Kill 'Em With Kindness-Selena Gomez
    7) Apocalypse-Cigarettes After Sex
    8) Silence-Marshmello, Khalid
    9) Bloodline-Ariana Grande
    10) Trouble-Valerie Broussard

1
THE DEVIL
IGNAZIO

Everlasting fucking gobstopping, mother of fuck. I was just starting to unwind when the marinara began shimmering. Of fucking course, my damned cell interrupts my fucking solace. For the love of Christ, I just wanted one night to relax, make some fucking delicious ass pasta and have a nice evening with my family. I should have known it was too much to fucking ask for. The ball breaking call has my jaw clenching as my irritation grows. There's no fucking way this is going to be good news, it never is… especially at this ungodly fucking hour.

"Fuck! Junior come stir the sauce." My older brother groans his annoyance loudly as he wheels over from the living room to the stove.

"Language!" Ma yells back at me from the couch where my family is gathered to watch the game.

"Yeah, yeah. Sorry, Ma. I need to get this." I lift my phone up for emphasis before stepping out onto the patio and taking in the splendid view of the harbor.

"Ciao, Enzo. How ya doin'? How's the family?"

"Ciao, Piromane. Good, good, they're good. Listen… I got something for you to take care of. It's heading in your direction. Get pest control on it. Capiche?" Hell, spazzing fuck, just what I needed.

"Capiche." I confirm, holding onto my composure by a thread. Just fucking wonderful. Looks like I'm exterminating some poor fucking piece of gutter scum tonight.

"Christ on a fucking cracker!" I run my hand down my tired face as an alert goes off on my phone. The text provides a photo of the idiotic snitch who must have steel in his balls to rob a notorious mobster. It also provides the address of where he was last seen. The snitch fucker's dealer is less than fifteen miles away. This disrespectful crack peddling pubic hair has me fucked up... all kinds of fucked up. I'm in sadist mode, with fury pumping my adrenaline up. An internal firestorm starts fuming from my anger. I need to get that brain scrambling shit off my streets.

I don't just live in the city of Baltimore. I own it. I've got my fucking territory on lockdown. My eyes are fucking everywhere. Not a goddamned thing happens without me knowing about it. When issues occur, I deal with them by taking a very hands-on approach.

Of course, there are some who find my tactics to be too demonic for their tastes. I've developed a reputation for being the goddamned devil of the underworld. The rumors that I've brought demons here to corrupt souls have spread like wildfire. Total bullshit, of course. Although, there is no denying that our society has lost some of their moral sanity. Violence has become second nature; it's even ingrained in our upbringing. Taught and handed down from generation to generation until it became our very own language. It's the reason that the people here rely on me. It's their only hope of protection from the truly demented jizz stains who slip through the cracks with copers.

This oddity fuckfest wasn't always my destiny. It was

meant for Junior, but that shit changed when he lost his legs in Afghanistan. I assumed he would resent me or at least want to kick my ass when he got back. Instead, Junior came back traumatized, haunted by the torture he endured. He never spoke about what happened there. He refuses to.

I was twenty-five when I started running the family business, and I've somehow managed to not fuck up for a decade while maintaining our empire with a solid reputation that still incites fear and demands respect.

"Luca... Paolo, suit up. We're rolling out in ten."

"You boys need to eat something before you leave."

"Sorry, Ma, we got to go."

"Oh, hush. I won't hear any of that nonsense. My boys aren't leaving without anything to eat. You all need your strength. I'll have some cold cuts made in no time." I glance at my Rolex impatiently as I wait on my brothers and our sandwiches to be ready.

I notice Junior sitting by the stove with his eyes glued to the Raven's game. I swear, fucking every damned thing is out to piss me off today. "Junior 'ey...keep stirring. It's going to stick." I snap, gaining his reluctant attention.

"Alright. Alright. I'm stirring, I'm stirring. Stop bustin' my balls."

"Surprise...motherfucker!" I walk in playfully, not getting much of a reaction. Ray's eyes only look up for a moment before returning to the blank wall in front of him.

"Get your chicken fucking, hick ass up! You're screwed. I know you've been staining my streets with fucking chiva." The punk ass fucktard surprises the shit out of me and

Paolo by responding with a massive grin. That's a fucking new one. It makes me and my brother share a puzzled look.

"Yo, Goondola, 'ey...you hear me, you fuck!?" I'm losing my damn patience with this dickwad. I aggressively snap my fingers several times in front of his dazed face. It takes me back a bit when he hardly reacts.

All the junkie scum manages to do is lightly giggle. "Bro, he's fuckin' out of it." Paolo states the fucking obvious with a hint of amusement.

I shake my head, observing several puncture marks and bruises between his fingers and lining his forearms. "Yeah, the fuck must have just popped a needle. Tracks are fresh."

"Let 'em chase the dragon. He'll still feel pain. It will be a fun challenge." Paolo rubs his hands together maliciously as the cruel wheels spin in his devious mind.

"You're a twisted fucker, bro."

"Back at ya. Let's see if our pal still feels numb when a slug hits his foot." Paolo aims his Glock before letting it pop off.

"Fuck! Fu-ck!" That did the trick. Ray is alert as fuck now. He whimpers when he spots his blood gushing out of the hole in his shoe.

His cries of pain keep getting louder and louder. The pathetic wailing is insufferable. I'm about to kill this cock juggling weasel myself if he doesn't shut the fuck up. "Enough!" I warn him with a deadly glare that has him trembling.

"Wh-wh, wh-at, is this?" He looks around at one of the trap houses he owns, confusion written all over his face.

"This...is your eviction notice. Don't return to my city. Fucking, ever! Capiche?" His body is shaking as I approach him and plant a kiss on his forehead. I walk away with his phone, finding a massive directory of clients before locating the name Alessandro. Paolo hangs back to remind ol' Ray here of the consequences, just in case my seal of death wasn't fucking clear enough.

"Yes-yes, I'll go. I'll go now." He shakes his head rapidly, twitching erratically as the urgency to flee pulses through what is left of his defense mechanisms.

"What's the rush? We were just starting to have fun and you want to leave?" Paolo taunts him in a polite sing-songy way, flashing the dirtbag a haunting smirk.

"Come on, I'm fucking bleeding, man. My foot is killing me. It's only drugs. I'm just selling drugs." He whines out in a desperate plead that fires my violent tendencies into motion.

I grab the fucker's nose, tightening my fist into a firm grip. "You got that shit in high schools. A dozen fucking teens overdosed last month. That's on you, you sick fuck!" I hiss furiously as I crack his nose.

"Fuck! Fuck, you, y-ou broke it. You broke my nose. I-I'm just trying to be like you guys. Build something, ya' know?" This gutter trash fucking tweaker has tapped into my last goddamned nerve.

"Hmmm, Ray still doesn't get it. Paolo, you wanna help him out with that?"

"Love to. You'll *see* things clearly real soon." He delivers this dark promise with a sinister smile.

Paolo goes to his toolkit to pick out a brand of torture worthy of such an occasion. He goes with a sharp scalpel that reflects the lights in the room as it slices off the miserable son of a bitch's right eyelid. His pain leeches out

2

BAD BLOOD
STELLA

The morning shines brightly on my face, stunning my overly sleepy eyes and causing me to squeeze them shut against the glare.

"Arrrrgh, why...why is this happening to me?"

I hunt down the possessed contraption that woke me up with my hand under my sheets. Looking at the screen makes me want to scream. It seems as if I just fell asleep moments ago.

Last night I received a massive last-minute order for two-hundred shirts with my saw scaled viper cocoon design on them. I'm pretty sure that the members of the Save The Snakes organization missed what I was going for. The design is meant to symbolize the metamorphosis of a soul turning to the dark side. But the only thing that matters to me is that they loved it. Their order couldn't have come at a better time. Now, I can pay my bills on time so that I can live on this expensive planet for another month.

It took pulling an all-nighter to get them done after I finally finished writing my Econ paper. Creating designs for my online clothing store, Sweet Apocalypse, is my biggest passion, and doing it full time is the dream. The screen-printing process, however, can be time consuming. It's frustrating and awkward to do alone. I need to have one hand holding the screen down while I balance my hip to hold the other side in place. When I'm using my squeegee, I hold my breath and stay as still as possible. It's my 'don't fuck it up' ritual. I can't afford to use more materials if I do mess up.

It's always a serious struggle for me to manage everything in my life. I really needed at least four hours of sleep to function. I guess I'll have to find a way to manage on fumes. I'm just not sure I can keep going like this without burning out.

"Hey, Mom. What's going on?" I answer the call hesitantly. I'm not able to roll my eyes hard enough. There is no way to prepare for a conversation with my mother. I know that it will surely test my sanity. It takes everything in me to not ask her what she wants since she never calls unless she needs something.

"Finally...I thought you would never answer. I'm seriously concerned about your reputation. You know... it doesn't just affect you? You're making me look bad, too. You've been single for so long that people are starting to think things." Here we go on this bullshit again, it doesn't surprise me it's just super disappointing when it comes from my mom.

I'll never measure up to the fictional version of my sister that she's built in her head. She compares everything I do to how Saverina would have done it. It's an endless punishment.

It isn't the only way the death of my sister still torments me. She was only six years old when we found out that she had acute promyelocytic leukemia. I was the only one in our family who was a genetic match. When Saverina's kidneys failed, I didn't hesitate to give her one of mine.

Even with the immunosuppressive drugs, her body still rejected my kidney. I've been carrying around a strange guilt ever since.

"Luckily, I'm too busy studying to have time to care about my reputation." I spit out defensively, which causes me to hate myself deeply. Stupid instincts. I can't stand giving her the satisfaction of knowing that she got under my skin.

"Stella, I'm serious. I've had enough! You are going to stop wasting your time. It pains me to see you throwing your life away." *Throwing my life away? Urgggh!* I'm building a career and taking business classes to improve my sales. How in the hell is that a waste of time? She is constantly saying shit like this to try to control me. I've seen her manipulate everyone around her and it isn't going to work on me.

I force myself to take a moment and suck in a deep breath to stop myself from exploding. It will only put more tension into our already screwed-up relationship. Besides, I hate confrontation, especially when it comes to defending my dream. "Uh, speaking of pain... How is your back today?" I decide to take the high road by changing the subject and hopefully avoid getting any more hyper-critical judgment from her. I'm also trying to avoid a dose of her volatile anger.

My mom has been in chronic pain for as long as I can remember. It's torture for her and everyone around her. It has turned her into a spiteful, bitter person who thinks that world owes her something. She becomes truly demonic, fury erupting like a volcano when things don't go her way.

"Oh, Stella. I can't believe I almost forgot to tell you... I bumped into Raymond Costa the other day. Domenico is single. Can you believe it? He's always been so handsome... and he is *very* well off." She masterfully changes the subject with the worst lie and topic ever. There is no way that she almost forgot, and I know she remembers everything Domenico has done to me.

"Mom, I..." I pause to collect myself before I say something I can't take back. It takes several deep breaths to reign in my crazy. I don't have words for the freakshow she is trying to put on. She knows damn well that Domenico is a sexual predator. I've seen her witness his vulgar and perverted behavior countless times. It started with him sexually harassing me and it has gone on for years. I can't stand to think of how my parents never did anything about it. Especially when I was a minor.

"What? Stella, wh-at? You need a husband and Domenico is willing to marry you. You should be grateful!" It's such a good thing that you can't smack someone through a phone.

"I don't want a husband!" I snap as my temper heats up at her wild expectations. It gives me some sort of sick satisfaction to deflate her hopes. I do love the idea of being in love, it just isn't conceivable for me. In my family, love is used as a weapon.

"You don't know what you want or what is good for you. You're a disaster. I don't see how you haven't landed a doctor when you are so close to John Hopkins. Saverina would have been married ages ago." I try to calm myself by remembering that this is her fucked up way of making sure I don't settle like she did with my alcoholic father. But it would mean more to me if she were looking out for my best interests. Unfortunately, I know better by now. She wants me married to a man with deep pockets that she can reach into, and it's never going to happen. In fact, I've considered marrying a homeless person just to spite her.

I attempt to use the inherited skill of dodging unwanted subjects against her. "Have you heard from Al?" I ask her curiously since, I haven't talked to my brother in over three months. The sad thing is that I'm used to it. He doesn't always have a phone and the number is always changing when he does. He isn't even on social media. He says he's on strike from using it until everyone gets back on myspace. So, that's never going to happen.

"You mean since he stole my jewelry?" She hisses contentiously.

I love my brother, flaws and all. He's my blood. I would do anything for him, and I have. Believe me. But he's an addict with several dangerous vices. I'm always worried about where he is or who he is with, wondering if he's hurt or maybe even dead.

My jaw clenches and I furiously shake my head. "Yeah... since then." I spit out harshly. All I want to know is if my brother is alright and all she cares about is her damn jewelry. She is so heartless. It pisses me off so much. Al could be in serious trouble. He's always getting himself into bad situations.

"Oh, Stella... dear, listen, I've got to go. I'll ring you later. Smooches." Yup, that seems about right. It's impossible to get her to talk about my brother for more than a few seconds. At least I didn't have to listen to her trash my father. That's always so much fun. It's never anything new, either. His day to day consists of drinking and sleeping. It's just so depressing and hopeless. No matter how hard I try, he always refuses to get help.

"Okay, later." My mom is such a piece of work, no wonder I'm such a hot mess.

Familiar purring comes from my window, signaling me that my little friend is on time for our breakfast date.

As I open the window, I hope this will be the day that Marlon feels welcome enough to pounce in here. He puts up with me petting him, showing mild annoyance with his eyes plastered to the counter. I giggle at him before turning around to get his food.

"Can you believe her, Marlon? Domenico is an evil predator! He's a walking sexual harassment case," I tell the cat as he devours the meow mix faster than I was able to get the can open. "She doesn't even care that he tried to rape me. It infuriates me that he got away with it after being caught by our waiter. He just laughed it off like it was a joke. Ugh, he's such a disgusting pig!" It suddenly occurs to me that Marlon is long gone and that I've been talking to myself the entire time. Awesome! This is a really good look for me. Maybe this is a sign I should go back to therapy. Nah. Sanity is overrated. Some of the best creative minds are batshit crazy by society's standards, and that doesn't sound so bad to me.

3
WHERE ARE YOU?
IGNAZIO

We all get into Luca's brand-new blue Salamanca hued Phantom Rolls we got him for his twenty-eighth birthday. I close my eyes, resting them, after giving Luca the address. Less than an hour later we find ourselves in front of a shabby house in Dunkirk.

The one-story brick house has a lake-sized dip in the middle of the lawn, with a hill on the driveway that is even steeper. Luca keeps the car running while Paolo and I carefully walk through the shadows. There are patches of woods between the house and the neighbors, which makes it easier for us to case the joint. The lights are off and there are no signs of movement inside.

Paolo picks the garage door open and we find a prehistoric 1986 Chrysler LeBaron Town and Country wagon parked inside. The maroon-colored paint is faded, and the side wood paneling is chipping. I'm not surprised to see it run down. It's rare to see one of these relics anywhere outside of a boneyard these days.

We head through the garage, gently opening the door that leads into a kitchen that reminds me of my favorite diner. I give Paolo a pointed gesture to follow the sounds of a television program being played in the near distance, and we cautiously split up.

While Paolo starts to search down here, I make my way upstairs. There are two doors in the middle of the hallway that branches to the left. I'm prepared, Glock in hand, as I open the first door slowly. Peeking inside, I find a closet filled with linens. The next door leads to a bathroom that smells way too much like a port-a-potty. I close the door as quietly and quickly as possible to lock the heinous scent in. Moving past the corner reveals three more rooms.

The first door leads to a bedroom where two people are sleeping. It's impossible to see if one of them is the filthy rat fuck or not because they're both covered under the bedding. I walk closer and lightly lift the blanket, and my feet shuffle frantically in retreat as I drop the bedding back into place. Holy... fucking balls. Someone fucking shot this broad up, real close and personal.

There is a corpse of a man next to her with his brains blown out. I'm not sure who these unfortunate fuckers are, but they're way too fucking old to be the vermin I'm looking for.

Sweet, baby Jesus... I need a fucking vacation. That thought runs on a loop through my head as I go to search the rest of the rooms.

As soon as I enter the next room, I flip the lights on and find the person I'm looking for in an unexpected state. Alessandro is shaking and sweating, a disoriented expression on his thin face as blood fills it with a dark hue. He's clearly drugged out of his mind. I begin to approach him with my gun steadily aimed at his skull. His whole fucking body starts seizing and his eyes roll back. Fuck. I need this fucker alive. He's the only one who knows where the money is. I approach him and turn his body to the side so he doesn't choke on his damned tongue.

"Don't fucking die!" It's a phrase I'm sure I haven't used before, but something deep inside me needs this fucker to hang on and I'm not sure it's just about the money.

"I-I-I...so, so sorry, Stel." His face becomes ghostly as his body falls limp.

"God fucking dammit!" I roar, loudly enough to grab Paolo's attention. Not even a moment later, I hear him running up the stairs. I look at Alessandro and shake my head in disappointment for some fucking reason. *Why couldn't you just keep your fucking trap shut? You, stupid, stupid fucker!*

Dammit! It never fucking fails, stupid motherfuckers will always do stupid fucking things. How am I going to find the money now?

Paolo rushes in, looking at me for direction with a panicked look before he sees Alessandro's body. "That him?" he asks, and I nod slightly. "Any last words, like a clue to where the fucking money is?" I shake my head as I scan the small room with my eyes.

"Search the house. We have to find it."

Paolo starts looking around the desolate room as I go to look behind the last door at the end of the hallway. I step inside a gothic inspired room with two matte black walls. One has a white castle twin bunk bed against it, which appears to have been made from plastic decades ago. There's a shabby dresser with missing knobs on the other side of the room and an intricately painted shelf hangs above it. I'm intrigued by the design. The design shows a gun shooting stars out into a dark sky. It's a stunning piece of artwork, and I can't fucking stand that it is slanted. It's a show of disrespect that irks the hell out of me. It pulls me closer, intrigued to see the picture that is barely balancing in the middle of it. I'm so stunned, I have to do a double take at the family photo to believe what my eyes are seeing is actually real. My shock doesn't come from seeing the three corpses I just looked at looking alive and happy. That's weird as fuck, but I'm too damn distracted by the bombshell in the center of the photo to register anything else. There she is, standing in the center of the universe, sparkling like the shiniest jewel earth has to offer.

Her beauty is so unbelievable that it's hard to see her as anything but a dream. Her photo is torturing me. Mesmerizing me. This raven-haired, smoking-hot vixen with her obsidian, come-fuck-me eyes and irresistible berry-stained lips has me hook, line, and sinker. Hell, just thinking about sucking on them has my cock waking the fuck up. *Who are you?* I take down the faded gold frame and bring it closer to my face before I removing the shelf and walk into the hallway. It's hard as fucking nails to shake the stabbing ache in my chest or the violent erection causing mayhem in my pants.

I haven't fucked a woman since I took over the family business. That hasn't stop them from fucking me, though, and they're always extremely grateful for the opportunity. They all bore me now, so I rarely accept their advances anymore. There's just no desire or thrill. Zero passion, just expectations for things a monster like me couldn't possibly provide. I'm not capable of the romantic shit, and nobody is going to change that. I'm sure as fuck not about to fold to this little temptress. I can't. Even if she does have some kind of dynamic pull over me that I don't understand. This is fucking unacceptable. Lord have mercy, this is fucking hell. This sexy vixen might be the only person with the power to take me down.

It takes way more self-control than I want to admit to put the mystery woman's picture in my backpack. My anger turns to rage that heightens the longer it takes to find anything. We've looked everywhere without any clue as to who this magnetic woman is. What I should be furious about is the fact that we can't find the damn money. It clearly isn't here. Paolo and I have searched the place a half dozen times already.

I go back to Alessandro's room to get his phone from his bed before I use his thumb to let me into it. Immediately, I pull up his texts and read the last one he sent. It's to someone named Stella, the name he spoke just before he died, and the message is lengthily.

I'm so sorry... so, so sorry. I know you're going to be mad. Please don't be mad. They were coming and they would have done worse. I had to save them... to save you. I had to. Go to the honeysuckle place and take the bag under the tire. Take it and go far, far away. As far away as you can. I always fuck everything up. I know that, but I just need you to trust me one last time. Go and be careful. I'm sorry that I was always a shit brother. I love you and I'm trying to make up for it now. Even if it doesn't seem like it. Fuck, Stella please just don't hate me.

Stella. The message was sent two hours ago and is marked as unread. *Stella, Stella, Stella.* My beautiful Stella. I bet you're sleeping peacefully.

It's excruciating to stay focused on the job at hand while fantasizing about Stella. I try to find her address in his cell but don't have any luck until I check his search history for shipments. Boom fucking shak-a-lacka, I've got it.

Before we split, Paolo and I spread a few bags of corn chips around to bust this joint with. Paolo empties another bag, spreading it in a line going through the garage that leads to the car. Once he's outside, I grab another bag of chips out of my backpack, along with my Zippo to light it with. I quickly toss it on top of the path of chips while standing in the doorway and watch as the oil from the chips works as a potent exhilarant. It spreads a trail of fire through the house, as powerful flames engulf the vehicle. Dancing with it in soothing, fluid motions that are addicting to watch.

"Fuck, Bro, we gotta go. Come on, you can light something else up later." I shake my head to break my daze. Paolo's right. We need to get on the road towards Towson. Although, it would be so much better if Stella could remain dreaming. The news I have to deliver is going to be worse than any fathomable nightmare.

4
WHATEVER IT TAKE
STELLA

Why? Why? I don't understand why the universe is so against me getting any sleep. The creaking sound from the front door opening forces me wide awake. Dammit, dammit, dammit. I shouldn't have forgotten to spray it with WD-40 so many times. The door startles me when it creaks again from closing.

I take a deep gulp, looking over at my window as my instincts contemplate fight or flight. My head whips around as my bedroom door opens and my options become slimmer. The dark silhouettes of three men stand in the doorway. All I can do is pretend to be asleep as two of the guys enter my room, getting closer every oxygen stealing second, until they reach my bed. My heart starts thumping wildly when one of them grabs my feet while the other goes for my arms.

I kick my right leg up and my foot makes jarring contact with someone's nose. "Fucking bitch broke my nose." The man holds onto his nose, jumping around in pain while the other guy starts tying my hands.

"Get the car ready and watch your fucking mouth... and

your fucking hands." The brassy sound of the baritone voice sends icy chills through my veins as heat spreads everywhere else. The wounded man holds onto his bloody nose, leaving his pride and a slew of curses behind him.

While the other man is securing my hands together, I throw my arms around his neck while wrapping my legs around him tightly to secure his body. I begin to choke him out as I struggle to hold him in place. He fights back hard, but eventually his head falls limp to the side. I'm quick to shove his body off me, looking up defensively. I relax slightly when I hear his body make a pounding noise when it hits the floor. Good. Two down. One to go.

The cryptic third man slowly enters the room just as I look up. When he steps into the light, my jaw drops open in shock. I'm stunned by how devastatingly handsome he is. His bright smile radiates charm with a comforting warmth. It's insanely disarming. Darkness dilates his pupils, shrouding them in mystery. I've never seen a more perfect looking man. It's shameless how distracted I am by this devilishly handsome stranger. I should be concentrating on finding a way to save myself. As he reaches the end of my bed, my survival instincts finally click in. I roll to the other side of my bed in a flash and spring out of it, ready to run like never before.

It's too late to give my feet a pep talk, though. The sexy beast is too close. He radiates some kind of powerful energy that terrifies me to my core, while also getting it drenched. I'm all over the place trying to get a grip on the situation as he stalks towards me with determination. I'm hanging onto my composure by a thread. The way he is looking at me is so intimate. It's as if he can see through my clothing and consume me with his intense predatory gaze alone. A crimson blush forces its way through my cheeks. I try not to gulp as I take in his size, considering how much larger he is to my own small frame. The tension in my throat becomes a slow sinking pain that travels from my throat to my stomach. That's it. I'm done for. He's built stronger than a damn brick wall.

I curse myself for looking up at him when I feel his gaze travel over me. My eyes lock with his dark ones, and I take the opportunity to carefully open my nightstand drawer. In one stealthy motion, he has our bodies pressed together. The dangerous man takes me completely by surprise when he gently touches the shell of my ear, taking his time to tuck my hair away.

"Stella. Stella," He whispers my name as if it's a revelation he can't stop repeating. Each time, his voice gets softer, drawing it out. It's so damned sexy. I'm devastated to find myself craving the sound of it. "Stella." I close my eyes, wishing I didn't want to hear it again so badly.

"That was very impressive kitten, but it's not going to work on me. You will be leaving with me." *Oh, hell to the no.* I frantically push him away with one hand as I use the other to pull the taser out of my drawer. I'm rushing nervously and my hand is shaking, but I still manage to zap it into the side of his ribcage. His body shakes but stays firmly rooted to the floor. The muscles in his jaw flex, his determined eyes never leaving mine. He just raises one eyebrow, daring me to make another move. If only I had one. Out of instinct, I search my surroundings for a solution.

He smoothly uses this opportunity to grab the taser from my hand and I groan out my frustration. My sound of distress only provokes him to taunt me with his dazzling smile, sending me into a state of confusion. It distracts me from noticing that his hand is on my throat until I feel his calloused thumb stroking my pulse. My heart and breathing take a rapid trip together as my traitorous hormones take over. Warm lips storm mine with a sweet cinnamon flavor that tingles against my lips as my mouth is furiously consumed. My eyes begin glossing over from lack of blinking. Biting back a moan makes me so proud of myself that I let his dominating tongue slide right in. I can't retreat yet I can hardly take it. This passionate frenzy has opened me up, leaving me vulnerable.

The heated kiss is hungry, insatiably intense. It makes me so lightheaded; I'm worried the room may start spinning if I don't do something. Anything. I squeeze my thighs tightly together, hoping it will help. It's no use, I just can't seem to help myself. It's not fair to be turned on this much by someone so dangerous. His lips pull back into a charismatic smirk that somehow almost makes me forget he is an insane criminal who just broke into my apartment.

"Fuck, kitten. There's more electricity in your lips than in your taser." I try to convince myself that this can't possibly be real life, when he drags his teeth down my throat slowly, his mouth sucking my throbbing pulse so hard that the blood under my skin boils to the surface. Wild sparks spread through my sex while my clit flutters, my breath unsteady.

"So fucking sweet," He groans into my flesh with a kiss. "I'm going to devour you when we get home." I squeal loudly as I'm turned upside down and thrown over the hot brute's shoulder. When I feel handcuffs clink on my wrists, I raise hell in any way I can, trying to get free. They don't stop me from pounding against his back with full force, but he doesn't even flinch.

My rusty front door squeaks closed behind us and the brisk fall air gives me chills. I watch as colorful leaves get crunched under his feet as my body bounces against his back. As soon as we get to the parking lot, I start screaming bloody murder.

"Help, I'm being raped!" I scream loudly, hoping

someone will come to help. Everyone just keeps walking. What the hell? Then I remember something I heard on the news once. "I mean fire! There's a fire!" I yell, hoping that those messed up statistics I heard about were correct and that my words get the attention of the few people I can see in the near distance. They still don't look over.

"No! No! Come back! Please!" All my hope flees when I hear a car door opening just as I'm placed on my feet. I turn my head at the unusual color choice these goons went with. It's like they give zero fucks about getting caught by the police. I roll my eyes at the flashy neon blue vehicle, showing my disdain. The dashing swindler seems to take note, chuckling as he shakes his head, causing the dark wave attached precisely to the side of his part to fall over his forehead.

He's so damn sexy that I'm worried my expression will give me away. "You can tell me what you prefer to ride on the way." I'm about to throw a truckload of sass in his direction when I notice the man in the driver's seat in my peripheral. He's holding a gun on me with one hand, the other holding a red handkerchief to his nose. His forehead wrinkles, a stern expression painted across his face. I take a deep gulp as he waves the gun through the air before pointing it at the back seat. I'm fighting tears when I slide into the car that will take me away from any semblance of safety. This cliché players club themed car is surely the first sign of bad things to come. I'm fiercely alert as the sexy mystery man scoots in next to me. Goosebumps rise above my skin as he wraps one of his arms around my shoulders casually as if he's done it dozens of times before.

His brow kicks up with interest as he studies me carefully. "Tasers are illegal in my city, kitten." Yeah? No, shit sherlock.

My eyes roam over his body with thick judgment.

"Hmm, and that outfit isn't?" I tilt my head sassily to provoke him before I look away, staring out the window as he laughs at my insult.

I feel his hand cup my cheek, guiding my attention back to him. He tilts my head up as he looks into my eyes dominantly. "Don't worry, kitten. I won't be wearing them long."

5
STELLAR
IGNAZIO

Luca pulls his car into the parking garage with the speakers blaring *Regulate* by Warren G and Nate Dogg. Luca has it turned up so loud that the beat is causing the whole vehicle to vibrate. Stella begins fidgeting nervously as she looks around. She seems so scared. I can't stand seeing her this way, it's giving me a strange pressure in my chest.

My brothers get out of the car and head into the elevator, finally leaving us alone.

"We're home." The words are meant to soothe her but instead they coax my demons to relax. There's something so soothing about having her here with me. It's the only place I know she will be safe, where I can keep her safe. This is where she belongs. Our home.

I recently acquired a luxury five-star hotel and renovated it into a home for my family. It's a soaring glass tower on the edge of the eastern harbor. We now live less than two minutes from little Italy, and it doesn't get much better than that. Well, in the states anyways.

The architect charged an arm and a leg to convert the former thirty floors into fourteen, but it was worth every penny and appendage. The new residence has everything one could ever need.

It has a massive garage, a reception area, employee residences, a lavish ballroom, a fine-dining Italian restaurant with two Michelin stars called La Madia, a gym, and a spa. All of which are solely run for my family.

There's also a floor stocked with our artillery and above that is our personal morgue. The morgue really comes in handy around here, where fishing, hunting, and construction thrive. Having the facilities make it possible for us to discreetly dispose of our enemies. Fuckers that can't touch us if we're in one of the safe rooms, which we have located on every floor. There is even an entire floor solely used as a designated safe space.

The remainder of the floors are lived in. Dante has the first residential floor, which I had adapted so there would be plenty of room for him to get around. He lives there with his wife Eve and my nieces Giada, Gabriella, and Giselle. My baby sister and youngest brother have the floors above him. My parent's floor is in the middle of ours and it's the grandest, of course. Then there's Matteo's but he hasn't seen it in person yet since he's been stationed in Germany for the past three years. Bria lives on the next floor up with her husband. Paolo and his wife have the floor above them.

Naturally, I chose the top floor and got it with ease. It's right below the outdoor pool and has the best views of charm city. My siblings all gave it their best when they arm wrestled me for it. I was very generous and even gave them best two out of three, but their guns were no match for mine. Not even close.

"Who are you? Why are you doing this?"

"My name is Ignazio Montague. That's all you need to know for now. There will be plenty of time to talk after we get settled in."

Stella backs up slowly, her body shivering as my name sinks in and I practically see the lightbulb go off when she realizes who I am. "I'm not going anywhere with you!"

"Have it your way, kitten." I scoop her up in my arms and take her inside the elevator. She struggles until we reach our floor and I remove her handcuffs. Stella huffs, walking towards the windows to take in the view of the waterfront lightly shining with the reflection of the moon.

"This is for your protection. Your brother could have gotten you killed."

"My brother? You know Alessandro?" Stella spins around abruptly and gives me an expectant look.

"Not well, no. I do know that he screwed over the wrong people and put a target on your head." I hiss the words out, thinking of the danger her shit for brains brother put her in.

"I-I-I have to call him and, and my parents." I can see the wheels in her head turning at an exhilarated rate, air escaping her body in panicked breaths. It's similar to the way I feel knowing what I must tell her next.

"Stella, he murdered your parents. It was a mercy kill. There were men he stole from who would have done horrible things," I tell her as calmly as I can manage. It kills me to cause her any amount of pain, let alone giving her news that is this excruciating.

"No! No. I don't believe you." Stella starts pounding her hands on my chest, and I wait for her to settle down before putting my hands over hers and gazing deeply into her mesmerizing eyes.

"I saw it. He overdosed. I-I couldn't stop it. He's gone. They're gone, Stella. Here... look for yourself." I pull out Stella's phone to show her the message her brother sent just before he died. She shakes her head, nibbling on her bottom lip as she reads it slowly.

"He... he really did it. They were all so, so... miserable. And toxic. I'm not sure how to feel. I don't even know if I feel sad. Not totally. Is that messed up?"

The question is spoken rhetorically, but I decide to respond anyway. "Not at all. They don't deserve it."

Stella looks at me, her big eyes gleaming innocently. "I still have to go please... you have to let me go home. Marlon needs me." My jaw clenches so tightly my teeth feel like they might fuse together.

"Who the fuck is Marlon?" I roar, sounding like the crazed maniac she's turned me into. Whoever this fucking Marlon guy is, he is dead meat. I will wipe him from her memory and this earthly plane for good if necessary. I am her future now.

Stella's face turns hard, all innocence gone from her expression. She looks like she's prepared for an epic battle. "He's a stray cat who will starve without me!" *A cat? It's a damn cat!?* I was jealous of a fucking cat. Fucking livid, a murderous rage boiling inside of me. I'm so relieved, I let out a sigh and my breathing returns to normal.

"He won't. Cats are predators... they're natural hunters." My assurance doesn't comfort her like I'd hoped. No, my words just set her off.

Her eyes shoot daggers at me. She is so fucking sexy with this little attitude of hers. She's putting my cock through hell. "You don't know him! He's old and squishy. Marlon relies on me." I chuckle at her attempts to persuade me to let her go. There isn't a force on this planet that would make me let her leave. Still, it's adorable. I lift her body up and carry her to our room before gently placing her on our bed.

Stella moves as far as she can on the bed, sprawling out against the mulberry silk sheets and looking like every man's wettest fucking dream. "Holy fuck," I groan, shaking my head, the mattress sinking under my weight as I crawl into bed. "You're so damn sexy!"

Fucking chump, get it together. I can't seem to find a shred of control as I slowly drag my eyes down her sinuous body, all the way from her doe eyes to her juicy, pillowed lips, dazed when I get to her gorgeous breasts. "Don't worry, I'm going to take good care of your kitty. You have my word and right now you're... getting my mouth."

Stella's lips part naturally as I hungrily lick my own. "What? Wh-at do you mean?" Her wholesomeness breaks me. I can't keep my debaucherous hands off her curvy body any longer. My hands start to explore her killer legs that feel so incredibly silky. The material of her panties feels so similar it takes me a second to figure out I've reached them. Feeling the wetness there puts a triumphant smile on my face. I groan loudly as I rip her panties from her sexy body and inhale her sweetness on them. Stella's eyes go pitch black as I lift her nightgown up, cursing under my breath at the prettiest little pussy ever created. It's shining for me like a flare, signaling me with its moisture to rescue it.

"It's been hell keeping my hands off you. My mouth deserves a reward." My mouth descends upon her swollen clit in a flash, running my tongue along her slit for a taste of the honey I'm insatiable for.

Stella's hands grip the sheets as I slide my tongue up and down her wet slit. My beast is uncaged, growling against her core wildly, devouring her harder with every moan she gives me. Those sexy little noises she's making drive straight to my hard-as-fuck cock. I'm filled with so much pride seeing her eyes fired up with lust and knowing it is all for me.

"Lose the bra, Stella. Show me those perfect, gorgeous tits." Stella looks reluctant at first, but she finally gives into her pleasure. She removes the black lace, tossing it carelessly to fall to the floor. I shake my head when she drapes her arm over her breasts, hiding them from me.

"Play with them, kitten... make them feel real good." Stella's face blushes as she begins to knead one breast, tweaking the nipple on the other. The hotter than hell sight has me half delirious and I'm sure that I'm salivating. They bounce when I grab her hips firmly to hold her in place for my tongue to run along her warm channel. I'm grinning widely into her little pink hole, pleased with the knowledge that the divine flavor of her pussy is all mine.

"Ignazio. Please...it's too much." That tells me it's not enough, but she's close. Come is leaking from my slit, I'm getting damn near close to losing my load as I pull her tight against my greedy mouth, my tongue picking up speed.

"Ignazio, I-I, Oh. Yes, yes." Stella erupts around my tongue with staggering moans as her body shatters.

I greedily lick my lips for every last drop of her sticky arousal. "Mmmm, you taste like the sweetest sin," I moan, fucking loving my new treat.

"Holy shit," Stella gasps as her head crashes down on her pillow. Her breathing begins to steady, slowly turning to light snores. When I'm sure she has fallen asleep, I head to the bathroom to take care of my tortured erection.

When I get back in bed, I pull out her phone to do a little research on my sexy little vixen. I send my sister a few pictures I nabbed from Stella's social media accounts, and after I'm done copying them to my phone, I delete them. My sanity doesn't need more eyes on her. Bria is beyond excited to meet Stella and happily agrees to come over tomorrow with a wardrobe. I will do anything and everything in my power to bring Stella happiness and pleasure. The moment I saw her it became my life's greatest mission.

6

KILL 'EM WITH KINDNESS
STELLA

"Iggy? Where are... oh. Hi, there. I'm Bria. I've heard so much about you."

"You have? From Iggy?" My amusement peaks as I look over at Ignazio, who is grinning from ear to ear.

"Oh, yeah. He can't shut up when it comes to you. He hates that nickname, by the way. So, of course I love it." We share a laugh that brings an enticing smile to Ignazio's handsome face.

"Iggy... What is all this?" I tease with a curious smile as I run my hand along the chic clothing on the rack. I've never seen such lush fabrics and designs in person. I'm sure the price tags would have me cringing and I'm relieved that they're no longer attached.

"I thought you might want to have some things to wear. Although, if you don't..." The wink he gives me sets me on fire. His striking appearance could get him out of anything.

Unless you're related to him. "Iggy!" It's really cute to see Ignazio's reaction to his sister's reprimand. He gives her a soft look and chuckles sheepishly.

"Where did it all come from?" I can't help but explore

each stunning item curiously before I can turn my head for a response.

"They're from our family's fashion line Amour Noir. The Montagne's flagship Boutique is just down the road." Bria informs me with a friendly smile as I hang on to every fascinating word.

"Are these your designs?" My eyes go wide at the creativity that was so obviously involved in designing such intricate pieces.

"No... Sadly, I don't have a creative bone in me," She laughs thinking about it. "They're mostly Ma's. Some of the pieces were designed by her and Carabelle. I run the business side." I nod, assuming Carabelle is yet another sibling. Damn. This family is huge. How can they stand being so close to each other all the time?

"They're gorgeous and very impressive!" She smiles proudly and it's obvious the pride isn't for herself. It's for her family members. It seems genuine, which kind of throws me off.

I suddenly feel super bad that she did so much for me, especially with her being very pregnant. "Oh, no! Did you carry all of this yourself?" The poor woman is waddling around, holding her back for support and looking thoroughly exhausted.

"Well, I was planning on it, but my husband wouldn't let me. Robert insisted on bringing it to the elevator. He's so sweet, but it wasn't necessary."

"It is, Bria. I want to see you taking it easy for the next month. Then you can go back to being super woman. Capiche?"

"Ah, I'll give you capiche." She moves her hand from her belly to slap the back of his head.

Ignazio laughs at her stubbornness, but then his expression turns serious. "Go, rest now. We will see you at dinner." I flash my head in his direction, shocked by his bold statement. I don't remember getting an invite nor do I recall accepting such an offer. I shake my head, deciding it's best to let that stew until his sister leaves.

"Alright, alright. The baby is hungry anyway. It was so nice meeting you, Stella."

"You, too. I look forward to talking with you more." I give her a warm smile as she goes to grab her forest green crocodile bag. Looking at it, I realize it is a designer bag, and I can't help thinking that it probably cost more than most people spend on their monthly bills. We wave goodbye and the moment she's out of sight, I spin around and glare at Ignazio.

"Dinner? That can't happen! Not that you asked. Big surprise there! I won't go. I won't. I hate family gatherings." I spit out, angry at the vulnerability in my voice. I squinch my eyes tightly shut, puckering my lips in distaste at the panicked words that escaped. I'm wracking my brain for a way to backpedal my way out of this conversation when I feel strong arms wrapping around me in a comforting hug and Ignazio presses me gently into his warm chest. I feel my eyes weakening as they lace with moisture. As much as I want to spin these feelings into anger, I can't. Ignazio's smell is calming and it's all around me. The combination of freshly laundered clothing, charred sandalwood, and a touch of a spicy citrus that reminds me of freshly grated ginger sizzling in oil makes me feel like I could stay here forever.

Ignazio caresses my hair as he leans in to whisper in my ear, his cinnamon breath warm against my cheek. "It won't be like that. I promise. We will have fun. There will be tons of good food and they will all *love* you." I feel ridiculous for being so dramatic. It's just a meal. All I need to do is be polite and get through it. An hour of family drama is totally manageable.

"Come on, kitten...let's see if it all fits." Ignazio gives me a devious grin, like he knows something that I don't.

When I pull a group of hangers off and drape them over my arm, I'm shocked at the weight. They didn't look this heavy. I readjust on my way to the bathroom... if you can even call it that. It's reminiscent of a scaled down St. Peter's Basilica. It's as if Michelangelo had been resurrected just to create it. The domed ceiling has a moon roof in its center, where the sun shines through to highlight the blue and gold mosaic panels. There are even intricate Corinthian columns adorning every corner. It is all over the top, totally unnecessary.

As I put on a linen, zebra-printed jumpsuit, I begin to wonder who Ignazio really is under his brutal reputation. I take a look in the mirror and hardly even recognize myself. So much has changed in the past twenty-four hours, even my appearance has become more classically suited to me. The drained and exhausted look is gone from my face.

I would trade in my normal t-shirt and jeans for this outfit. It's even comfortable. I swear, rich people get the best stuff. Even the hand soap in the bathroom feels luxurious, while smelling spectacular and gourmet.

I struggle not to become addicted to being pampered as I try on all the clothes. Ignazio insists on seeing everything I put on. It would bother me if the obvious appreciation in his eyes didn't make me feel like I was glowing. I pick out a bright red, puffy, long-sleeved chiffon blouse with a long bow draping down the center to wear with a pair of black tapered wool pants and matching ankle boots.

After I get out of the shower, I see loads of feminine products that weren't there before lining the counter. In the center is a white and beige leather chest with gold accents.

My curiosity has me sneaking over for a peek after I'm done drying off and changing into my outfit.

Ignazio walks in casually with a light smile before opening the box and pulling out one of the small drawers. He takes out a pair of ruby stud earrings that are surrounded by a circle of diamonds and hands them to me with a sweet smile on his face.

"This is... too much. It's just dinner. I couldn't."

"They're yours, kitten. If you don't wear them... no one else will." It unnerves me how sexy I find his dominance and possessiveness. It shouldn't have me fantasizing about the way his mouth felt when I orgasmed.

I desperately try to distract myself from the sexual tension building inside of me by playing with the bow of my blouse and crossing my legs. "What time is dinner?" I rasp, determined to get control over my hormones.

"We can head down at eight."

"Eight? Seriously?"

"Don't worry, kitten. I won't let you starve." Ignazio wets his lips suggestively and just like that, my pussy is fluttering back to life.

Ignazio shows me around his gigantic place, and I'm certain I will end up getting lost. Ignazio thinks it's hilarious when I request a map to not get lost. It's a real challenge, geography is a foreign concept to me.

My heart felt like it was going to explode when I noticed that he had the shelf I painted hanging in his office, along with the only photo in existence of my whole family. They were the only possessions that mattered to me inside the house I grew up in.

As I freshen up for dinner, my nerves have me on edge. I can't understand why I'm so worried about what his family will think of me. Ignazio links our hands as we head to the elevator. We arrive at the fancy restaurant on the third floor of his building, and I realize that it is likely only there to serve him and his family.

"Good evening." A friendly, middle-aged woman greets us enthusiastically.

"Good evening, Moira. Stella will be joining us from now on."

She gives him a nod and a courteous smile that spreads when she looks at me. "It's a pleasure to meet you," She greets me kindly.

"Thank you. It's nice meeting you as well. Wow this place is... it's... I don't have words."

She laughs for a moment, sharing my enthusiasm. "Dear, I still can't find them either," Her eyes glaze brightly as she cheerfully hums. "Wait until you see the palm room." We walk into the room we will be dining in, and I gasp. Moira was spot on. This is incredible. The dining area seems elegant enough for royals.

"Oh, wow!" When I look more closely at the burnt orange wallpaper, I see that the golden damask print has the most gorgeous sheen to it.

Moira gives me a knowing smile. "It's gorgeous, isn't it?" I nod at her before I look back at it. "I didn't even know wallpaper could be made from Italian silk until I saw it here."

I tilt my head curiously. "I didn't either. It's so beautiful."

"You're so fucking sexy when you get inspired." Ignazio kisses me on the cheek as he escorts me towards an oval table covered with a pristine white linen tablecloth. I instantly feel like I've somehow stained it just by looking at it. What's worse is everyone at the table is no longer distracted by their loud conversations. It is now deathly silent and it feels like a million eyes are piercing into me. I feel a small sense of relief when I see Bria's friendly face.

Ignazio brings me over to his parents who are seated in front of an intricate golden mirror with a laurel wreath crested on it. The middle of it is embossed with the initials D&G. The powerful statement piece fits the room perfectly, with its regal monarch crown standing out boldly at the top.

Ignazio's parents get up right away and hug me tenderly, giving each of my cheeks a brief kiss. I don't know if it's an ancestral instinct or not but I return the affection without thinking. Bria introduces me to Robert, who seems to be on high alert every time he looks at her belly. It's a level of protectiveness that I've never seen. I feel my eyes watering and bite my cheek to prevent the tears from falling. Ignazio pulls out a clementine hued velvet chair embellished with gold studs and motions for me to sit. He waits for me to sit down before gently pushing in my chair and taking the seat between me and Robert.

A cute little girl with raven-colored pigtails runs around the table in circles, causing everyone to laugh. She stops suddenly, looking at me curiously, and Ignazio lifts her onto his lap. "Gabby, what happens to runners?" She giggles softly and shakes her head.

His brow sharpens as his expression goes steely. Ignazio begins tickling her until she can hardly take the laughter anymore. She finally raises her hands in surrender so she can catch her breath. He puts her down and she returns to her seat between her older sister Giada and her stunning mother Eve, who Dante married straight out of high school. Dante gives her a sweet kiss on the forehead before returning his attention to his youngest daughter. She's reading something on a tablet, and he is patiently helping her pronounce any words she gets stuck on. I'm seated next to Paolo's wife, who is the perfect picture of a socialite who was groomed perfectly for the role of a polished and proper woman.

"Do you have any children?" I ask Valentina, trying to break the ice. I'm taken aback when she breaks into gales of laughter.

"Not a single one. Who has the time, Bella? Can you imagine?" I'm slightly annoyed by her forgetting my name already. She shares an amused look with Paolo and I suddenly feel like the clown in her personal circus. Meanwhile, Paolo just rolls his eyes, seeming bored by the whole interaction.

"Carra, did you know that *Stella* is a designer?" Bria remarks, dissolving the tension in my stomach. I don't think I could be more grateful to anyone than I am to her right now.

"I would love to see your designs." She tells me excitedly, causing her brilliant eyes to gleam. Something about her expression tells me she means it which makes me feel excited to share them with her.

"The whole world will soon. Her creativity has been hidden far too long." Ignazio shocks me with his intense statement, and somehow deep inside, I'm certain he means it.

7
APOCALYPSE
IGNAZIO

Stella's laughter brings a warmth to me that I feel deep inside my soul. I knew that she would fit seamlessly into my family. She is making me hope for things I've never dreamed of before. I'm committed to having everything with Stella. She has possessed me deeply and surrounded me in a peace I've never felt. This gorgeous vixen is running through my veins like an exhilarant. Burning there deeply, forging an unbreakable flame.

It's past eleven when we get back to my place. Italian meals aren't known for being short affairs. Stella climbs into bed after positioning her pillows just right.

"Where is the honeysuckle place?" I couldn't stop thinking about it all through dinner. I need to get that money before Enzo gets restless and sends in reinforcements.

Stella is distracted for a moment by a large yawn. "Huh, oh yeah... I'm not surprised Al picked that place. It's in Bladensburg at the old go-kart track. My family used to go there sometimes after mass. There's a stool made from a tire there that Alessandro would stand on while he lifted me up so I could get to the honeysuckles." Stella becomes lost in her bittersweet memories. It infuriates me that even this happy memory has now been tainted by her imbecile brother.

Stella rolls over onto her side as she adjusts her body under the covers. I pull her into my arms to comfort her, and she surprises me by leaning into me. A huge smile begins to creep over my face.

"Everything happens for a reason, baby. You were meant to live a much better life." And she will, from this day on. I won't let her go to bed with this sadness on her mind either.

"That's hard to believe sometimes. Sometimes I-I think that my sister had more potential. Maybe my family would have been different if it was me instead."

"No, baby...you aren't responsible for who they were as people. They would have been the same way with your sister. She went when it was her time and she's in a much better place."

I cover the side of her head with my hand as I slowly inch myself closer to her body until the tips of our noses are touching. "Look at me, Stella," I whisper, waiting until her smokey eyes are set on mine. "No one has more potential than you. No one."

Stella rolls her dynamic eyes at me and giggles sweetly. "Do you know what your greatest weapon is?"

"Sì. My Glock, firestorm. I keep it loaded with Smith & Wesson incendiary ammo that burns up to five-thousand degrees Fahrenheit, lighting a fire where it lands."

"So, it looks like a firestorm? Hmm, I'd love to see that sometime. It isn't your greatest weapon, though. No, your greatest weapon is your smile." I don't miss the flirtatious tone in her voice and my shaft sure as fuck doesn't either.

"How so?"

"When you smile, you're believable... everything doesn't seem like it's too good to be true."

"Then I will be doing it much more often." I wink at her and we share a smile.

"I need to know something."

"Go ahead. I have no secrets from you."

"Your thing with fire. Did it come from peer pressure to live up to the meaning of your name or something?"

This sassy side of hers amuses me to no end. It's like watching a maltese bark at a pit bull. I can't help myself from laughing while shaking my head at how adorable she is. "No, no, no, kitten. You've got it all wrong. Fire has a thing with *me*. Has since the day I came into this world. It could have taken my life before it began. My whole family, too. No one woke up to the smoke alarms except Ma who only woke up because her labor started. She was able to get everyone out in time."

"Wow, your mom is so incredible! And so talented."

"She thinks you're pretty fantastic, too. So does Dad. You know he's pretty talented, too. He recently started journaling his life story. Says he's going to be a famous author." Stella giggles at that thought. Probably picturing him signing books for fans. That would be a funny fucking sight.

"Isn't that kinda a bad idea in your profession?"

"It is. Try telling him that." I raise my brow sharply in a challenge while grinning at her response.

Stella looks at me like I suggested walking over hot coals. "No thanks. I'm good," A light yawn falls from her lips as her eyes droop a bit. I pull the feather comforter over us while Stella moves around and gets comfortable laying on her side. "Do you really think they liked me?" She turns her head back to read my expression in the sweetest way.

"Yes... of course they did. Baby, you're perfect. Try to tell me one flaw that you have. Try to lie to me. I dare you," I grunt against the shell of her ear, nipping at the cartilage there. "Fuck it, how about I show you?" I lift Stella's silk gown up over her head, letting loose a slew of curses under my breath as I take in her plump ass which is only slightly covered by a nude g-string.

"No more panties in bed." I command in a harsh grumble as I smack her perfect ass a few times to make sure my point has been made. Once I have her out of them, I become lost in my caveman lust. I lick my lips, gritting my teeth hard as I slide two fingers into her hot little pussy, my thumb sinking into her clit, rubbing the bundle of nerves with deep strokes. Stella's sweet gasps turn to erotic moans, causing my erection to jerk out of the opening in my boxer briefs. I use my free hand to seat my erection between her ass cheeks, pumping against the globes in a blissed-out mania.

"You like that... feeling how fucking hard you make me?" Her tight cunt pulses around my fingers, gripping them so firmly they can hardly move.

My primal instincts cause a growl to erupt from my chest, my body full of sexual rage. "Fuck, I need more room," I take Stella's leg and swing it around mine, and she hooks it around me as I keep a firm grip around her ass. "You're so damn tight... you're going to destroy my cock." I'm dying for the sensation of her vise like grip squeezing my cock.

"Ignazio," Stella gasps my name as my fingers pump in and out of her silky heat. I stroke her perky nipples and lay a trail of kisses up her neck.

"Ignazio... please,"

"Please, what? What does my sexy little kitten want?"

"I-I, I need to..." I lay a trail of tender kisses across her shoulder blade.

"Mmmm," Fuck, Stella's sobs are so exquisite. I could listen to her pleasure forever.

"I know what you need and I'm the only one who can give it to you." I jolt my fingers into her core, hitting her g-spot in deep circles as I press harder against her clit. I feel her clenching my fingers as she goes silent for a beat before breathing out in desperation. I'm breathing hard in a flash, screaming her name as I spill my seed, marking her backside.

Stella looks completely exhausted, letting out a few satisfied noises between yawns. I kiss her cheek lovingly while gently running my hands through her smooth hair. "Sweet dreams, baby."

"Mm, sweet dreams, Ign-azio." She yawns my name out so sweetly I'm tempted to pull her closer and fall asleep with her in my arms before I clean her up. It takes a lot of willpower but I force myself to get up and go to the bathroom. I grab a washcloth and wet it with warm water to clean my girl off with. Once I'm done, I've resolved that this will be the last time my seed doesn't go where it belongs.

As soon as I wake up, I send Luca and Paolo to go retrieve the money. While they're doing that, Stella and I pack for Carrabelle's wedding, which I've done my best to prevent from happening. There isn't anything that could change it now. It's a done deal. My father still has the last word and he's dead set on this fucking wedding happening. To him it's the only thing that will keep our allegiance strong in Miami, and that is all he can see. He's blind to all the things Carrabelle is giving up.

We get to the airport bright and early, and Stella gawks at our private plane, looking as though she's never flown before. My curiosity is piqued by her apparent nervousness. "Is this your *first* time, kitten?" Stella nods, nervously biting her lip. My cock jerks wildly as I pull her onto my lap and wrap my arms around her protectively.

"As long as I'm on this earth, there isn't a thing that can hurt you. You became my whole life from the moment I first saw your picture," I cup her face as I try to show her how much she means to me. "Stella, I love you." I kiss her passionately, feeling a painful pleasure run through my cock.

"I need you... I need to make you mine. So fucking badly."

I yank the front of her magenta dress down so aggressively the straps break, causing her gorgeous tits to spill out. My hungry eyes roam over her voluptuous breasts. The sexy sight has me packing a fully loaded gun in my pants, and I feel like I've been electrocuted when a slight turbulence causes them to jiggle.

"How are you so goddamned beautiful? I can't keep my eyes off you," I groan, feeling my chest rumble as I slide my thumbs over her nipples, hardening them into stiff peaks.

"How are you so charming and sweet? It's hard to see you as a killer." I can't help but chuckle at her adorable expression. She's lost in her thoughts, clearly shocked from her confession. I lift her chin up pointedly, a raging inferno blaring through me.

"You will... if anyone ever tries to hurt you. There isn't a soul alive that I wouldn't incinerate for causing you any amount of pain."

8
SILENCE
STELLA

"*You will... if anyone ever tries to hurt you. There isn't a soul alive that I wouldn't incinerate for causing you any amount of pain.*" Ignazio's wild eyes are giving me goosebumps, his words ringing in my head. My sex has somehow developed its own heartbeat. Tingles spread throughout my body when I feel his hard length jerk against me. Ignazio cups my ass with his hands, pulling me up, and I instinctively wrap my legs around him as he carries me down the aisle of the plane.

He opens a small door that leads to a luxurious bedroom. It's at least two times the size of my bedroom at my apartment. Before I can gather my thoughts to think straight, my dress and panties are on the floor and Ignazio has me pinned down on the bed.

A hint of dominance plays across his sinful face as he removes his white boxer briefs, letting his monstrous cock jump out aggressively. My jaw drops and I shake my head in disbelief. Ignazio is huge... way too big. No way! Nuh-uh.

"I can't wait to hear you scream my name. First, you're gonna tell me, kitten... tell me you need me," Ignazio starts teasing my clit with the head of his shaft. It feels so good, so insanely right that my body feels fully alive for the first time. "Tell me who you belong to." Ignazio's possessive dominance radiates through his richly seductive words. His voice has a hardened edge that drives me wild.

I'm overpowered by my hormones; their intensity has me lost somewhere in space. "I-I, I'm please... fuck, yes." I'm so turned on, I've lost the ability to speak properly.

"Tell me, Stella." His dark eyes heat into mine, demanding and pleading at the same time.

I've gone completely mental, my body twisting needily to make contact with his. "I'm yours." I speak the truth, unable to deny anything with my libido running rampant.

"Your little kitty doesn't need to be scared. Trust me, you're going to love every inch." Ignazio runs his enormous shaft all over my sex, sending shivers down my spine. He could make me come just by doing this. Seeing his devilish eyes riveted on my body, I melt for him. I can't help it... I'm molten wax under his hard body. It's such an incredible turn on to be the object of his desires.

"Look into my eyes, Stella." His stern words make my hormones pool in my stomach. My body tinges with heat when I see the way his eyes pierce into mine.

"You're my whole life. I'm going to marry you... going to give you so many babies." Ignazio's dead serious, I feel it in my gut. My blood pressure must be off the charts from feeling his monster thrust inside of me.

The deep connection changes everything in an instant. Our hearts are strangely drumming in unison. "You were made to be mine, Stella. It's why your body feels like coming home. It's why I need you so much... why I need you all the damn time." Ignazio's sultry eyes are locked on mine. It feels like all the oxygen in the room has been sucked out as I feel his erection growing inside of me.

His hard length plunges deeply, firing my erogenous

zones with electric sparks. "Ignazio, fuck... yes." A fusing euphoria ignites my entire body. I'm so deeply consumed by the explosion; black spots start to appear in my vision as my head slams down on the pillow. I can't stop my limbs from trembling. Feeling Ignazio's warm arousal shooting through me is extremely addicting. My pussy is greedily draining every drop it can get. I'm left completely exhausted and deliriously sated as I lay my body across Ignazio's perfectly sculpted muscles that flex as he squeezes me closer.

It takes getting to our hotel for reality to fully hit me, and I start to freak out a little bit. I'm going to be attending his sister's wedding in just a few hours. It's a big deal. I'll be meeting even more of his family members, after a ceremony that is going to go on for eons with extensive prayers and all the songs. Most of which will sound like complete gibberish to me since they will most likely be in Italian. This is probably the only time that I will be grateful for not being able to understand the beautiful language.

After taking a hot, lengthy shower, I'm feeling a million times better with a brand-new attitude. I've never been to North Carolina. I'm going to let go and have a good time. I might as well; I'm on vacation, even if it is a forced one. A vacay is still a vacay.

Of course, Ignazio used his cunning charm to convince me to close my online shop for a week. He's so slick. It's slightly terrifying. He made it impossible to refuse the top of the line, industrial screen printer he bought me when he saw my eyes light up at the sight of it. If that wasn't enough, it came with a promise of unlimited assistance from the sexiest man alive. Even the biggest fool alive couldn't turn that down.

9
BLOODLINE
IGNAZIO

We are in Asheville, North Carolina, where Carrabelle is being married off to Rocco Levi. The fuckwad's father happens to be the boss of Miami where Rocco reigns as his underboss. My father's gained their apparent loyalty through uniting our families. I still don't buy it, though, not even as we take our seats in the front of Basilica of St. Lawrence for the wedding.

The cathedral doors open at the back of the room, showing my nieces lined up in their matching dresses. Gabby walks down first, throwing her petals at the guests while her sisters scatter theirs on the floor. The ring bearer starts marching down the aisle, looking almost as annoyed to be here as I am. The wedding party follows behind him, getting into their positions. Everyone stands when they hear the opening bars to the Bridal Chorus. My father is smiling proudly down at Carrabelle when he offers his arm for her to take. I've never seen him as emotional as when he walks her toward the altar. He kisses her on both cheeks before giving her away to a family I don't trust.

The longer the ceremony goes on, the harder it becomes

to keep my mouth shut. I can't let this fucking asswipe marry my baby sister.

"If anyone here objects to the union between this man and this woman, speak now or forever hold your peace." My infernal rage boils to the surface, determined to stop this fucking abomination from happening. Before my demonic side unleashes, the church doors slam open. The guests who were in high spirits just a moment ago are now fighting to catch their breaths, paling from the shocking entrance that Timur Fedorov just made. Gasps and gunshots burst through the room.

Timur storms inside the church, looking like a maniac. It's slightly amusing to see the shell-shocked expression on Rocco's face before it's replaced with vile fury. "Do you know who the fuck I am? What you've done showing up like this?" Rocco screams, aggressively moving towards Timur. His face turns an embarrassed mottled red from having his reputation tested.

Everything after that happens in a flash. My adrenaline detonates as my survival instincts kick into high alert. I nod to my brothers and father to signal them to get our family out of here.

My father gives me a stern look that creases the wrinkles in his forehead as he pats my shoulder. "You too," His tone is so firm and definite that I can't say shit outta' respect. Fuck. I give him a hesitant look, fighting to keep my mouth sealed. "This is for me to deal with," he commands.

I look over at my life's greatest purpose and, without wasting another second, pick her up and follow my family out of the church. Hysteria is breaking out everywhere, groups of people running around in every direction. It isn't easy but I'm able to get my family out and secured in our SUV's. Before I go back inside, I can't fight the urge to claim

Stella's lips with my own. Her sweet mouth brings me peace, a moment of heaven, before all hell breaks loose.

Once I'm back inside, I start looking for my sister, who I can't seem to find anywhere. The sounds of three shots firing in my father's direction diverts my alarmed attention towards Rocco. The scornful bastard looks truly unhinged, laughing manically as he lays on the floor, holding onto his bleeding chest. This fucking dingleberry has some fucking nerve turning his twisted expression towards me.

A slimy grin takes over his face as he scratches the side of his head with his pistol. "Hmm, what a conundrum... we have here."

His fucking bird brain pauses in deep thought. It must be a real fucking struggle for this douchebag fucker. He stalls further by clicking his tongue obnoxiously. "This won't do," he sighs, pulling the gun away from his head and aiming it right at my father.

My temper explodes. "You're fucking dead!" I roar thunderously, raring to rip this fucker's fucking head clean off his body.

"Those were just some warning shots, bro. You know how it is. I *was* promised a wife. You fucking... owe me!" I want to take my Glock out and fill him with lead, but to say I'm surrounded would be a severe understatement.

"Drop it. We will get her back." I tell him calmly, trying to settle him down enough to reason with him. This damned bozo fucker is real fucking lucky that I'm appeasing my father's wishes.

"It's too bad your other sister is used." He spits out venomously.

That's fucking it. Fuck my father's wishes. Fuck respect. "You motherfucking prick fucker," I yell violently, running after Rocco as he makes his escape. I'm so fucking enraged right now; I can feel it sizzling in my bones. It doesn't take me long to realize how fucking fortunate I am to be safe right now, after I foolishly left myself vulnerable. After I left Stella vulnerable. That fucking shit won't ever happen again. I love my father, but I will never let his decisions jeopardize the safety of the future mother of my children. Never again. If he was anyone else, he'd be facing deadly fucking consequences right now.

10
TROUBLE
STELLA

Luca is hyper focused as he drives out of the parking lot like a maniac. Dante and Eve are comforting their girls, who are rightfully terrified. All I've been told is that we are going to an ally's home for safety. Paolo is following us with his wife, Bria, Robert, and Mrs. Montagne.

Finally, we park in the driveway of a Tudor style mansion. It's so grandly opulent that it outshines all the other houses in the neighborhood by a long shot.

Paolo and Luca leave immediately to meet up with their father and Ignazio. It's hard to swallow the notion that Ignazio could be hurt. Not knowing if he's okay makes me conjure all kinds of horrible possibilities. My thoughts are so distressing, I feel like I'm being sucked into a depressing abyss.

A blonde glamazonian opens the door, welcoming all of us in with a friendly smile. Everyone greets her with familiarity before I'm introduced to Gaia. We walk in the grand interior of the home, where a girl walks into the room to greet us. It's slightly humorous that, Cettina seems to be the pre-teen version of Gaia. It seems impossible to imagine this tough woman as a vulnerable, insecure person in any other way than through her sister.

Robert and Mrs. Montagne help Bria upstairs so she can rest, while Dante and his wife take their children to the guest suite to get settled in.

I can't bring myself to leave the couch or to stop staring at the door expectantly. Intense eyes size me up from the other side of the room. "Cettina, be a sweetheart and get our guest something to drink?" Gaia's words sound so sweet they barely register as a command.

"Sure thing," her sister responds with a knowing look before standing up. She starts to leave the room but turns back and looks at me. "How long are you all staying, anyway?"

"Until they're not anymore. Now go." Gaia responds sternly, giving a playful wave to encourage Cettina to go.

A sleazy looking, middle-aged man comes strolling in with an arrogant demeanor, and my nose is immediately assaulted by the foul odor coming off his body. The offensive combination of cigarettes, hard booze, and sour sweat, all coated with cheap cologne, makes me want to hurl my guts all over the half-zipped velour suit he's wearing over his hairy chest. "Sup? Stella, is it? You'se a real good looker, doll."

Gaia shakes her head at him in a chilling warning. "Fuck off, Tommy!" She shouts, scolding him like a child.

"Hey now, we we're just talkin' a bit. Isn't that right, baby?" He puts his grubby hand behind my shoulders so quickly I don't have a chance to react before Gaia does.

"Tommy, you fucktard ignoramus. That's Ignazio's girl." She informs him with amusement, and his arm whips back to his side. He starts to shake with nerves.

"Shit... shit... shit. I didn't... I didn't know. I was just trying to be friendly is all." He goes on the defensive, pleading with terror filled eyes.

"Get outta here, you gar-bage fuck!" He shoots up immediately, leaving the room as quickly as he can, without another word or look in my direction.

The room goes silent for a moment as I consider if I should thank her for getting that creep away from me. I'm beyond thankful to breathe fresh air again.

"Sorry... my Pa hires dickwads exclusively. Are you okay?"

"Hmm, yeah. It isn't him so much. I'm still just a little shaken up. I've never been to a wedding like that."

"Don't worry, they'll get those fuckers to tell them where she is. Carra will be home in no time at all." Her words of assurance do nothing to relieve my worries. I feel a deep dread building in my stomach from the unknown. Not too long ago, all I wanted was to get away from Ignazio. Now, my only wish in the world is for him to come back to me in one piece.

11
PLAY WITH FIRE
IGNAZIO

Paolo managed to detain one of Timur's men, but he got a little carried away. The stubborn fuck has had his face punched in a few too many times. It's pretty mangled, but the fucker wouldn't answer, so Paolo just kept pounding. We've dragged the cocksucker to the nearest motel and have him tied to a chair. Paolo went to the nearest hardware store to get supplies. I'm waiting for this schmuck to wake up when I realize who he is.

Konstantin fucking Kramarov. He is truly a fucking schmuck. The kind of filth who brags about selling drugs to children. A prideful guido-esque imbecile known for throwing obscene amounts of cocaine on his hookers. Something he calls getting a blow job for a blow job.

I am not a patient man and it isn't helping that Paolo is taking forever. It's beginning to piss me off. That's fucking it. I'm not waiting any longer for some goddamned answers. I grab the ice bucket, fill it with water, and pour it over the fucker's head.

Konstantin begins to stir but goes in and out of consciousness. Fuck that, he is going to stay awake. Out of instinct, I throw the ice bucket at his head. That fully rouses him, and I glare as he blinks at me with confusion. "Where is Carrabelle?" I roar aggressively, wishing I could rip his throat out to get the answers I need.

"I-I-I don't know, I swear." His eyes are stark with pure terror, trying to hide the fact that he's lying.

"See this gun? I'm going to teach you how to be real fucking honest with this motherfucking gun!" I slap him in the face with the side of the barrel to make my point perfectly clear.

He groans from the impact, causing me to growl with irritation. "You're okay."

Konstantin spits out blood before wiping his mouth and looking up at me. "Nyet." He hisses painfully. This weak fucker is pushing every single one of my buttons.

"No. What I said is you *are* okay! Trust me Kramarov, you haven't felt real pain yet."

He tries to act tough, pressing his lips together like they're sealed. Clearly this fucker doesn't know who the fuck he is dealing with. "You wanna die? Okay," I taunt him by drawing out each word. "I would love to introduce you to your maker. Hmmm... Where do you think that bright light is going to take you?"

"I told you... I know nothing." The bonehead fucker cries pathetically. I hear my phone ding and check the notification. It's from Paolo, telling me he is pulling into the motel.

"Wrong answer. Wanna guess who just got back with something real special?" I give Konstantin a malicious glare that he cowardly refuses to meet.

My brother walks in with our new purchase, and I look over at him. "Paolo, we're having a BBQ," He laughs hysterically at Konstantin, eyeing him intently as he plugs in our new, free standing infrared electrical patio heater. "It's so hard to get a tan this time of year. Let's help our pal get some color." Paolo chuckles through harsh coughs. He clears his throat, nodding as he makes his way over. We take the asshole from the chair, containing him as he struggles for freedom. Paolo holds him in place while I tie Konstantin's body to the heater.

"Still trying to remember? Okay. Let's see what happens when you start to feel fifteen thousand watts burning into your flesh." I turn the heater on, instantly seeing a thin layer of sweat along his upper lip as he gulps down his fear.

"Can you feel it already? The heat radiates almost instantaneously. It will sear your clothing next. Then the metal plate will burn holes into your flesh until it turns into blisters that will start to melt. Fat and blood will spill out."

"Enough, enough... I'll talk! Fuck, I'll talk. I'll tell you everything. Please just fucking turn it off!"

Smoke drifts up from behind his back as I turn the heater off. "It... it was revenge on Sylvester for killing Timur's family," he gasps. "Timur was just supposed to kill him and get out. I-I don't know why he took your sister."

"Convenient... But I know that you know where he took her."

"H-he, he didn't tell me," When I turn the heater back on, he begins screeching louder than a newborn. "Nyet, nyet... I really don't know. I mean it. I don't know. I don't know!"

"Yo, what's the latest?" Luca rushes in with concern for our sister, ignoring the hysterical fucker in front of him.

"Fucker won't fucking talk." Screams of terror wail from Konstantin's dirty mouth as he dies keeping Timur's secrets.

My family took Stella back to our home in Maryland. My brothers and I are helping my father search for Carrabelle. We've looked everywhere without any luck. It's been a whole goddamn month; the longest, most excruciating fucking month of my life. It took a lot of patience, talking through negotiations with Timur that evolved into verbal threats. A truce was finally formed when he sent my family proof of Rocco's death, but it took more than a fucking finger to get me to come around. It wasn't until I saw how happy my little sister was that I was actually convinced Timur was a decent guy. Not that I'm fucking openly welcoming him into my family or embracing him with open arms any fucking time soon.

When I get back to my Stella, I finally feel free again. My aching shaft is desperate for the same feeling. I've missed how crazy she makes me. I'm burning for her so intensely my nerves heat through my skin. My testosterone revs, causing deep growls to emanate from my chest.

"Ignazio, I-I-I was so worried!" Stella dashes towards me, pushing me slightly back with her firm hug before she jumps up, wrapping her juicy thighs around me.

My shaft is raging in my pants, throbbing painfully as it desperately attempts to break out. In a soft caress, I run the pad of my thumb over her plump lips that infatuate me to no end. "Fuck, kitten... I missed you, every damn second." My ravenous lips take hers in a fever frenzy so hot my cock begins to drip, leaving the head sticky, warm, and needy. Her lush fucking lips instantly pull me into a passionate craze. My mouth is lost in its devotion to Stella. I know I'm far past obsession at this point. Without even trying, Stella could get the most powerful man alive to willingly give up control.

I have us naked in bed so fast you'd think my life depended on it. I'm not so fucking sure it doesn't. Heaven comes to earth when Stella wraps her soft hand around my cock, teasing it slowly as she guides me towards her golden pussy. I've never been harder in my entire fucking life. My intense need for Stella is instinctual. With extreme urgency I shove my way inside her tight little hole. God, I fucking love the way her face flushes with passion as her luminous eyes glaze over with lust.

Stella's fingers dig sharply into my shoulders, causing euphoric pain. "O-oh, Ig, Ignazio," Stella stammers as I thrust in and out of her tight heat. She begins rolling her hips, deliciously playing with me as she grinds against my body, her cries of pleasure stirring something manic in me.

Suddenly, I'm struck by the thought of Stella with another man. It hits me harder than a fucking train and has me fuming with rage. A dark force rises inside of me.

"I'm never letting you go. You belong with me!" I pound into her hard, owning every inch of her slick center. I've never claimed to be a good man but I know I'll be fucking good for Stella. My need to protect her, to love her with everything I have and everything I am, has no bounds.

"So, good... so, so, mmm," Stella screams, and I feel her squeezing vibrations coursing around my length. I brutally capture her electric lips and my favorite buzz runs through my veins.

My hips buck as I snap, becoming a possessive animal. "Stella, I can't fucking live without you. I won't!" My declaration is firm and final. I don't want to consider what my life would be like without her. My world would burn down to crisp ashes.

Stella's body trembles as her tight sex grips me in waves. Our lips are still lost in lust as it breaks and we're both gasping for air. Stella's alluring mouth is a fucking sight to see, all swollen and cherry stained from our love. I'm a fucking delirious disaster, moaning heavily and pumping as fast as humanly possible when my orgasm bursts into live wired pulses that electrocute me from the inside out.

In this perfect moment, I'm only capable of communicating through growls. I've never come so hard or so fucking long. It's hotter than sin. "Fuck, kitten. I can't stop filling you up." As soon as my load is spent, my fucking cock is back to being erect. The way Stella orgasms is seared into my memory as the most amazing thing I've ever witnessed.

LUCIFER
IGNAZIO

I've been trying to catch that sly little bastard Marlon for weeks now. The fucker was supposed to be a wedding gift to my wife, but somehow, he's the only fucker alive who can evade me. I've lost my ever-loving fucking patience at this point. This shit ends today.

I've filled Stella's old apartment with things to entice the feline bastard. The window is lined with tons of catnip. I left it open to let the smells from the treats inside lure the scoundrel to me once and for all. I even set out a bowl of cream, along with a bowl of organic salmon. Don't fucking get me started on this picky fucker. Salmon almost got him once, but the fucker turned his nose up at it last second. I was so fucking pissed. Apparently, farm raised isn't fucking good enough but living in the fucking streets is just fine. What the fuck ever. This is where we fucking are.

I know I've gone a bit overboard. What can I say? I'm fucking bullheaded and fiercely determined. This place is no longer even an apartment. It's turned into a certified cat resort. I bought a variety of beds and toys, including a wooden tree that Jeremy at the pet store raved about like a fucking evangelist talking about God. None of this shit is fucking working. At this point, I'm actually contemplating throwing treats around the space like fucking confetti. A loud knock at the door takes me out of my ridiculous train of thought.

"Open up, Stella."

"Who is it?" I shout through the door.

"Domenico." He blurts with annoyance.

I open the creaky door to find some dumb shit meathead standing in front of me. He begins looking inside like he owns the fucking place. Finally, his eyes give up and reach mine.

"Who the fuck are you? Where's Stella?" His brazen questions wipe away every trace of my sanity. All I want to do is rip his fucking lips off his smug fucking face so he can never speak my wife's name again.

Deep fury unleashes my wildly possessive tendencies to the surface, and my face twists into a deliberately cruel look designed to make fuckers like this beg for their lives. "She's at home...waiting for my cock. Can I take a message?" My taunt is meant to be vicious enough to knock him down verbally before I lose control physically.

"That fucking... cock tease," he hisses under his breath, setting me off like a bomb. I yank the fucker inside by his shirt, throwing him harshly to the ground. The little piss ant gets up quickly, taking a moment to catch his breath. He must be a real dumb fuck because he starts to come for me. It's comical how easily I'm going to wipe his miserable existence away. I pull out my Glock and I'm ready to shoot the fuckhead, when Marlon practically flies through the window, wrapping himself around the idiot's head. I'm so surprised and the sight is so fucking ridiculous, I start to laugh. Marlon is really fucking going to town, scratching the ever living shit out of his face. The fucker screeches when the cat's razor-sharp claws dig into his eyes. He finally gets a good grip on Marlon and throws him to the ground. The cat hisses with a threatening glare, before turning his hungered attention to his personal buffet. I've clearly lost my sidekick, so I rush the fucking douchebag to the ground, slamming my rock-hard fists into his greaseball face until he's knocked the fuck out.

"You're both coming with me." I announce triumphantly, shutting the window.

I'm going to need some help before the fucker wakes up. I put a call into Paolo, who is waiting in the car with Luca. "Get in here... both of you'se. And come heavy."

Paolo and Luca help me get Marlon and dead man walking back to the house. On the ride over, Marlon sits on my lap, purring contentedly the entire time. We seemed to have reached some kind of mutual understanding, both of us wanting to see this cretin fucker gone for good. The deadbeat shit for brains should never have fucking mentioned his cock and the love of my life in the same sentence.

I turn the cremation chamber down to its lowest setting. My brothers and I lift the body, trapping it inside as the door closes and the lock clicks. My brothers decide to leave and skip out on watching the fiery show, but it's just too good for me to miss. It starts with watching his body contort into a boxer-like stance through the glass, fists clenched tight as his knees and elbows flex. As soon as the door was closed behind him, he woke up and I know he's in hellacious pain feeling every single one of his nerves scorching through the limbs in his body. It's a gruesome, slow as fuck torture that he will be conscious of almost the entire time.

Right about now his organs should be beginning to cook, and when they do, he'll be able to smell it. His nerve endings should all be dead, which means soon his fat is going to break down, his skin turning to leather as it begins to peal back. Boils begin to cover his body as his clothes fuse to the flesh that remains. At this point, his dipshit brain has likely gone into shock, taking him away from his excruciating end. The worst is over but it's still far from done. A howling wail erupts out of him when his body bursts into flames. Now he has the eternal hellfire of damnation to look forward to.

Marlon and I share a satisfied look, both of us feeling a fuck of a lot better. I take the elevator home, feeling impatient the entire time. I'm dying to see my wife's reaction. She doesn't disappoint.

Stella bursts into tears of joy when she sees us. "Ignazio...I-I can't believe he came with you." A huge celebratory grin takes over my face as I see my gorgeous Stella looking at Marlon, tender joy written all over her face. It makes me feel like the luckiest fucker alive because I was the one to make her million-dollar smile come to life.

"Mmm...I did," I give her a devious smirk. "And now, *you're* going to come with me."

O.D.D
STELLA-FIVE YEARS LATER

People have straight up asked me if I'm crazy for marrying Ignazio. I tell that I'm certifiable with a sweet laugh. There isn't a reason for me to explain myself. Ignazio makes me deliriously happy. He brought me out of a life that was draining me. I've never been so surrounded with support and love. It was overwhelming at first. I kept waiting for the other shoe to drop. My life still doesn't seem real. It's incredibly suspenseful. It might be twisted but, I wouldn't have it any other way.

I've hired two very caffeinated employees to help my ever-growing company with production, shipping and occasional coffee runs. Sweet Apocalypse and Amour Noir have a collaboration store that started as a pop-up called Sweet Amour. It's the best way to describe the way his family loves me and our children.

I left our employees with plenty of Ceremony coffee to roast so I could get out of the city with my family for the weekend. This is the first time I've experienced the apparent phenomenon of *glamping*. This is supposed to help us unwind a bit. I'm all about peace and quiet, but must it be accompanied by wildlife?

Ignazio starts building a fire with our oldest child and I'm trying to keep my eyes on our most mischievous one.

"Pour the chips out... spread them around." Ignazio instructs Stefano on how to use potato chips as kindling while I apply my fifth layer of bug spray.

Once the fire gets going, Ignazio gives our daughter a sack of elements that will change the color of the flames. "Throw the magic powder in, sweet pea," he coaxes. Mia throws a sack into the pit with wonder. She squeals in excitement when the fire turns purple, the heat reacting with the potassium chloride. The flames quickly turn back to their natural color, and Mia pouts. Her expression turns giddy again when Ignazio hands her another bag after giving Stefano his. I pick one at random that ends up being magnesium sulfate. We watch it turn the flames white before the kids throw in their last ones. Stefano's makes a deep red hue from the strontium chloride inside, and Mia's had the copper chloride which turns the blaze bright blue.

Ignazio and I get comfortable by the fire. He puts his arm around me, and we watch our children play. When they tire, Stefano crawls in my lap and rests his head in the crook of my neck. It's pretty adorable to see Ignazio's reaction when his son steals my attention. Both of us laugh when we see Mia rushing over to us, her doll like eyes gleaming hopefully. Ignazio raises his brow, stoically waiting for her to ask for something we all know she's going to get. It's impossible with my husband. He spoils her rotten. Okay, okay. We both do. We desperately need to find a way to take control, to be the parents, but come on! Those sweet little innocent eyes, those adorable dimples, and that irresistible smile she gets from her dad make it very difficult.

Mia giggles and starts throwing marshmallows at us, a

goofy smile spreading across her chubby cheeks. "S'more pretty fire? Please? Pleeeeeease," she whines adorably. Yup... she's definitely her daddy's girl. We are in such big trouble.

FORBIDDEN MUSE

I'm singing my biggest hit for the billionth time when my gaze meets a pair of rich hazel eyes that shine brighter than the most precious metal. The romantic lyrics of my song feel truly meaningful for the very first time. My heart and soul begin pouring out of me through every word. This seductress is way too young, too tempting, and too precious to be starring in my filthiest fantasies. It doesn't matter though; she became mine the second she flashed her flirtatious smile at me. That smile is driving me to act on my most basic urges. I refuse to let anyone or anything hold me back. My passionate serenade turns into a heated, seductive performance. It's just the two of us lost in this euphoric trance. Then, within the blink of an eye, she is taken away from me. My soul was soaring in her presence, but in her absence, it is crashing to the ground, shattering into a million pieces. Her father is a ruthless, powerful man who will stop at nothing to keep her from me. But he's in for a rude awakening. He's about to learn that not even a Mafia King can stop a Rock-and-Roll God when he's found his eternal muse.

SOUNDTRACK:
1. "Dream On" – Aerosmith
2. "Dream A Little Dream of Me" – The Mamas and The Papas
3. "Devil's Advocate" – The Neighbourhood
4. "Talk" – Hozier
5. "Rhythm Divine" – Enrique Iglesias
6. "SOS" – James Arthur
7. "We Belong Together" – Ritchie Valens
8. "My Girl" – The Temptations
9. "Heroes (We Could Be)" – Alesso ft. Tove Lo
10. "Wild Love" (Jonas Blue Remix) – James Bay
11. "Isn't She Lovely" – Stevie Wonder
12. "Celebration" – Kool & The Gang

12

DREAM ON
MAVERICK

I'm sitting in my dressing room feeling depleted from my tour and looking at the dark circles under my puffy, exhausted eyes. I've avoided taking a break for far too long and it's showing, big time. A vacation always sounds great until I consider the fact that I have no one to go on vacation with. My brother, Cortez, and his family are the only family I have left, but he's busy with his own life, and his family hardly travels. I'm not proud of the options I have left once I discount Cortez.

I have a few friends I used to be close to, guys I met in college. They still act like they're pledging a fraternity. Not too long after I made it big, they started seeing me as their own personal social ladder and an ATM machine. One whose name they could drop to book tables at exclusive restaurants and VIP sections at various clubs. Hell, I've even heard them drop my name to pick up women. I shouldn't have stayed friends with them for as long as I have. But I am loyal to the bone, making it difficult to cut strings with people.

These days, my best friend is my bodyguard, Rhett Anderson. I know he thinks of me as more than just his boss, but I'm sure he would much rather get away from the cameras for a while than vacation with a celebrity. I imagine protecting people from fanatics must be a taxing, obnoxious job.

"Surprise! What do you think of this, big boy?" I nearly go blind from shock as a woman pops out from behind the leather sofa where she had apparently been hiding. She shimmies her body, a contorted twisting motion that looks painful and is more than a little disturbing to witness.

"Rhett!" I call loudly as I use my chair as a shield. He rushes in and looks around, spotting the woman flashing me her naked body from under a bubblegum-pink trench coat.

"Ma'am, please cover up. Or shall we add indecent exposure to your trespassing charges?" he asks, earning him an outraged gasp from our uninvited guest.

She gapes at him, looking offended. She snaps her mouth shut, huffing and fuming as she covers herself, tying the belt around her waist. "Ma'am? Ma'am? Seriously!? I'm twenty-two!"

Rhett ignores her as he walks over and snaps a pair of handcuffs around her wrists.

"Can't we work something out?" She winks at me, sloppily running her tongue around her lips. I roll my eyes and turn away to look for my phone so I can call my agent, Ari, for an impromptu conversation. If this isn't the universe giving me a sign, I don't know what is. I pull up his number and initiate a video call.

Ari answers on the fifth ring. I assume he sits and counts because he *always* picks up on the fifth ring. He considers it his signature move. It's his little way of communicating how important and busy he is. He thinks it tells his clients that while he may be busy, he's never too busy for them. It's annoying, clever, utterly ridiculous, and just one of the many reasons he is so successful. The man truly is an enigma.

"This is my last tour," I immediately inform him when he picks up, my tone stern.

"You always say that. You don't mean it." Manipulation is a second language to him, just like it is for most agents. I consider ignoring him and hanging up.

Deciding that I need to make sure he's clear on my intentions, I say, "I do mean it. I will finish the final leg, and then I'm done. Until further notice, I am a recording artist and that is all I am." I've never been this blunt with him and maybe that's the problem. Maybe that's why I keep agreeing to these insanely long tours against my better judgment.

"Fine, fine. We'll talk about it when the tour is over." The cockiness in his tone annoys me, and his eye roll infuriates me. I'm about to hang up when he starts speaking again. "In the meantime, Ignazio Montagne has invited you to perform at a party celebrating his wedding anniversary next month." This fucking guy. He clearly isn't giving up. Didn't even hear me, I'm sure. Fucking typical. Ari only hears what he wants to. He only listens when there's money to be made.

Everything about what he just said is a straight-up no for me. I would think my agent of over a decade would know me well enough to know that. "Ari, you know that I don't do private performances. Especially not for a party, and *especially* not for a party of mobsters. What, are trying to get me murdered? Am I not making you enough money?" I'm genuinely curious to hear what he's thinking. The man is an eccentric genius, not a moron. He must have a good reason for making such a preposterous suggestion.

"Don't be dramatic, Maverick. It's going to be advertised. There will be cameras every-fucking-where. It's one song at a private party for a million bucks. Simple! Plus, this lineup is bigger than Bonnaroo. I'm talking big names here, kid."

"Yeah? Like who?"

"The Kings of Lions are going to be there. You love those guys."

"Ummm... Kings of Leon? I do love *those* guys."

He ignores my sarcasm and I roll my eyes as he continues. "There are going to be so many legends there. Like that phenomenon group, One J. They're reuniting for this performance." I wonder if the rest of his clients spend as much time wondering if he's having a stroke as I do.

"One... Jay?"

"Yeah bro, you know, One Injunction. They had the best song ever." Ari is one of the most brilliant men I know, but he comes up with the weirdest shit. I can't help but wonder if he says this shit on purpose so he can see if his clients are willing to indulge his crazy.

"Um... sure. Right." *I guess I'm boarding this crazy train with him.* "Who else?"

"Dashboard Professionals. You toured with them in ninety-four." We've worked with *Dashboard Confessionals* on several occasions. Who the fuck are Dashboard Professionals?

I attempt to jog his memory, even though I'm convinced he's just fucking with me. Yeah, we did an album with Dashboard. What the hell are you smoking these days?" Whatever it is, I'm sure he got it from his shaman, and I know that shit isn't legal.

"Yup, those were good times, my dude. Eh, eh, eh..." he chuckles himself into a coughing fit. Once he's recovered, he answers my question. "Don't worry your pretty little face over it, kid. You've never heard of this shit, but it's good, I promise."

"Sounds really safe, Ari."

"No doubt, no doubt. Kid, you know safety is very important to me." I *don't* know that. In fact, he's proven to me time and time again just how little regard he has for danger.

"So, just one song?"

"That's all, my man. All the artists are just performing one single. Ignazio made a play list for his wife. It's in the email I just sent." I sit down in front of my laptop and pull up the email.

Montagne Wedding Anniversary Play-list

"Stolen" – Dashboard Confessional
"Eyes On You" – Kings Of Leon
"Only You" – Maverick Siciliano
"One Thing" – One Direction
"Every Time I Close My Eyes" – Babyface, Kenny G
"Mercy" – Shawn Mendes
"Wild Love" – James Bay
"The One" – Kodaline
"Locked Out of Heaven" – Bruno Mars

Wow. That is one hell of a lineup, I think.

"Okay... I'll do it," I reluctantly agree.

"That's sick, kid! Solid, solid choice." I sure fucking hope so. I'm used to going with my gut when making decisions, yet for some reason I just can't get a read on it today. Too late now. I told Ari I'd do it, so it's a done deal. Whether it was the right decision or not, well, I guess I'll find out.

13
DREAM A LITTLE DREAM OF ME
MIA

I'm having so much fun getting ready for my parent's anniversary with my family. My mom was so patient and helpful when I tried on dozens of couture gowns. We both smiled when I twirled around in the dress I'd chosen. The perfect dress. It was from Aunt Carra's collection. The gown is deep-red and form-fitting and is strapless on one side with a frilly sleeve on the other. It showed just the slightest hint of cleavage, making it the perfect combination of sexy and classy.

Aunt Bria spent forever doing my hair and make-up to get it just right. It's weird to see myself so made up, but I love it. I smile at how mature I look as I run my hands over my curves. I take one last look in the mirror and wonder if I look good enough to catch the attention of someone famous. Not just any famous person, though. The only celebrity I have ever really wanted. I wish I'd been able to keep my feelings for him a secret. My family thinks it's just some silly crush. But they're wrong. I adore him. I always have, ever since the first time I heard him sing.

Maverick. I breathe in his name, savoring it. Siciliano. I exhale his last name in a rush. The calming tactic I've used to help calm me down for years doesn't work tonight. I'm still a bit dizzy. I find myself doing it again, chasing the crazy high that saying his name gives me.

Concerts are on the long list of events that I'm generally not allowed to attend, but I've noticed my father making some concessions ever since I started waving my age card around like a freedom flag when I turned eighteen. I'm almost nineteen, but I think tonight is proof that he's finally beginning to accept my independence.

"Mia, you need to change," my brother Stefano, who is older than me by one measly year, commands. I am so sick of him acting like he's the boss just because he's the oldest.

"What? No! I am not changing!" Out of all the males in my family, I have the easiest time putting my foot down with Stefano. At his core, he is basically a teddy bear. I know when he won't bend and generally give in on those rare occasions. I can tell this is one of those, but way too much effort went into picking the perfect dress. There is no way I am changing.

It's too late though, he's in my head and he knows it, if the cocky grin on his face is any indication. "Why, does it look bad? *Dammit. Dammit. Dammit. Why did he have to put doubts in my head?*

"Change," my younger brother, Roque, pipes in as he strolls into my room. *Ugh! He is such a tyrant.*

"Ugh, I hate having brothers!" I shout.

"What's up?" Cruze peaks his nosey head in, making me want to scream even louder. I'm never going to get any privacy around here.

"We're telling Mia she needs to change her dress." Stefano gestures in my direction and Roque seethes. I can tell he is still bitter that I'm going at all. *It isn't safe. It isn't smart.* His stern words ring in my head like a damn bell.

"Word, and you should," Cruze snickers at me, causing

my brothers to laugh together. I shut them down real quick with a piercing stare I've mastered over the years. When you have five brothers and strength isn't on your side, you need to develop some survival tactics.

"Change?" I snap. Cruze tries to interrupt, infuriating me further. "You'll have to rip it off my dead body!" I threaten, my tone serious.

"Mia. Stop fucking around. I said change. Now change," Roque says, sounding bored.

"Fuck off, Roque! Ugh, I can't stand you guys sometimes." I stomp out of my bedroom, frantically searching for my mom.

"Can you please get your goons off me?" I shout as soon as I find her in the bedroom she shares with Dad, launching myself into her arms. Like always, her embrace comforts me, but I'm still enraged.

"Oh, geez...What is going on now?" she asks calmly as she continues to hug me, leaning back slightly to try and read my expression.

"My dress." I leave her arms to twirl around before dramatically flopping back on her bed. My dad walks in, staring at me with wide eyes before giving my mom a pointed look.

"What dress? That dress? Is that even a dress? No, no... No way. That is what this is," he states firmly. Great. Just perfect. I get to go through another round of this crap. I just can't wait to hear more.

My mom huffs at him, rolling her eyes. "I showed you a picture of the dress a month ago. You were perfectly fine with it then," Mom reminds him. Hearing this gives me a sliver of hope. False hope, most likely.

"With someone else's daughter wearing it," he grumbles. I can tell that he's just toying with my mom at this point but am unsure as to whether he is going to try to make me change.

"That's very misleading. I'll remember that later." Dad nips mom's earlobe, and I grimace, desperate to get away from their lovey-dovey crap. This just went to the top of the list of things to talk about with my therapist.

"I'm sure you can be reasonable, Iggy," she implores, pouting playfully.

My mom has put in a valiant effort, but this is so not how I'm winning this battle. Building off the foundation she's built, I pull out the big guns. I take a second to straighten my shoulders and tilt my head to each side, gearing up for my take down. I'm pissed that it had to come to this. My mascara isn't even waterproof, but sacrificing my make-up for my outfit is the only solution available to me at this point. I only need to remind myself a half-dozen times that it will be worth it. I notice my brothers standing in the doorway and give them a smug little smile.

"I-I-I suppose Stefano was right. I'm just too fat to wear this dress. I should give it to someone attractive, like Roque said," I whine, laying the tears on thick. The extra drama is only heightening the joy I feel at seeing my brothers squirm. My dad is too busy glaring daggers at them to notice the glee I'm struggling to hide.

"Mia is the only girl beautiful enough for this dress. It was decided months ago by her mother and her aunts that she would wear this dress, and I agree with their decision. Have some respect. That is her dress. End of discussion," Dad declares.

Of course, Roque chooses to ignore Dad's warning to drop the subject. That boy lives to rebel against our father. "With all due respect, sir... I just think that – " Dad slices his hand through the air, cutting him off with a steely look.

Stefano and Cruze start pushing Roque out of the room. "End of discussion means end of discussion, son," Cruze mocks. Roque glares daggers at me and I bite my lip to stop myself from laughing at my younger brother's temper..

14
DEVIL'S ADVOCATE
MAVERICK

The guitarist that has been hired for the evening is Cam Meizer, an experimental artist who prefers not to commit to one band or label. "My manager just got me a deal that is going to take my career to the next level. I'm going to be the next Yogi." His statement came out of nowhere and confuses me. A few other people glance over before dismissing him and going back to whatever they were doing.

Bruno gives him the interest he was looking for with a pat on the shoulder. "So, are you going to be playing with the Yankees or are you becoming smarter than the average bear?" he jokes, and I chuckle.

"Hey, hey, hey! Jealousy is very cute on you. Baseball? No, no. It's so sweaty and... gross. I'm getting an-i-mat-ed!" *Getting?* I've never witnessed someone who fits the definition of the word better than this guy does.

I tune out the rest of the conversation, feeling nauseous from hanging out with the rest of the talent in the green room. Most of them are smoking various substances, adding to the thick fog in the room. The performances haven't started yet and there are two acts up before me. I'm feeling impatient, ready to get this performance over with. I really don't feel like singing this song for the umpteenth time. As far as I'm concerned, the lyrics to "Only You" are just one big pile of suck. The title alone makes me cringe. Yet here we are, ten years later and my fans still fucking love it.

I step out into the hallway to get some fresh air and see a couple of young women down at the very end, looking at the posters for the event. More specifically, the one with my face on it.

"He so doesn't look like he's close to forty to me." The echo from the hallway carries their voices, making it so I can hear every word clearly. I laugh in my head, thinking about how weird it is that even with Snapchat and Instagram, people fail to realize how much filters, make-up, special lighting, and Photoshop goes into making celebrities look amazing.

"He probably gets Botox. Who cares how old he is anyway! He is *soooo* hot!"

"Gabby, Giselle, shut up! Someone could hear us! He could find out what you said. Maverick is a musical genius. Please just... have some respect." The words are spoken by someone around the corner, someone I can't see from my vantage point.

I find myself moving closer, needing to lay eyes on the face with the most incredible voice, the voice of an angel. Just the sound of it has me turned on... and not just in a sexual way. My heart and mind are racing in tandem, both completely focused on the mystery woman. Everything inside of me is calling out for her. A woman I've never even laid eyes on. I can't believe the way I'm reacting to her, the primal urges that her voice set off inside of me.

I begin walking more quickly to reach her, but it seems like the hallway is getting longer with every step I take.

"Oh, puh-lease. Don't be a buzz kill, Mia. Even if he did hear what we said, why should he care?"

"Mia, snap out of it. One-D is about to go on." They move around the corner, and I continue to follow their voices. I reach the corner and search for the woman with the voice, the one whose name is Mia, apparently. Before I can find her, I hear a throat clear, and I look over at the young man trying to get my attention.

"Umm, sorry. You seemed to be daydreaming and I didn't want to startle you. I'm Stefano Montagne. My parents were wondering if they could meet you before you go on." He's so polite, I don't even know how to respond. It certainly isn't how I'd expect the head of a criminal empire's son to sound.

"Oh, um... sure. Nice to meet you, Stefano. Please, lead the way."

I follow Stefano down a different hallway and into the elegant restaurant, La Madia. It's furnished with rich orange and gold accents, and in the back is a small stage with a few rows of auditorium seating. We approach the front row and I spot Ignazio and a woman I assume to be his wife. They hear us coming and turn their heads, offering me warm smiles.

"Thank you for coming tonight. This is my wife, Stella," Ignazio tells me proudly, confident in the fact that he requires no introduction.

"Thank you for inviting me. It's really nice meeting you both."

"We're really looking forward to your performance," Ignazio says. His cultured tone and refined appearance are misleading. You would never suspect that he is the head of one of the largest criminal empires in the country. He's well-dressed, his tailored black and red pin-striped suit making him appear more civilized than I know him to be. Nobody would ever see this guy coming for them.

"Our family loves your music! Especially our daughter, Mia. She is probably your biggest fan. She would love to meet you. Maybe after your performance. If you have time, that is." Stella says, graciously giving me the opportunity to refuse.

I'm speechless with hope. *Mia. Mia? Mia is their daughter? She's my biggest fan?* I grow excited, knowing I might get to meet the angel with the amazing voice, and hearing that she is a fan. I shake my head in an effort to clear my thoughts, knowing it could be interpreted as a slight if I don't respond.

"I would love to meet her," I say, attempting to hide my excitement. I realize my attempt has failed when Ignazio gives me the evil eye, his expression knowing. I try harder to appear aloof when I say, "I'd like to thank my biggest fan." I breathe a sigh of relief when his glare melts away and he gives me a polite nod.

"That would make Mia so happy!" Stella's voice rises in excitement, and it brings a smile to my face. Hearing that I can do something to bring Mia joy keeps it plastered there.

15
TALK
MIA

Maverick overhears every word my cousins have said as he approaches us, and they both run off and leave me alone, giggling the whole time. He moves closer, pressing his chest against my heaving breasts as he lifts my chin ever so slightly; I savor his touch, the way it causes my skin to tingle. "I don't, by the way." His voice is so sexy, and I gulp as my hormones pledge allegiance to him.

My brow lifts as I try to remember what I was talking to my cousins about. "Huh?"

Maverick grins, his disposition utterly charming, seducing me without even trying. "Use Botox." He raises his eyebrows, causing the wrinkles in his forehead to deepen. For anyone else, showing off their wrinkles would be a horrible attempt at flirtation, but I've been following Maverick for years and I know that he has only gotten sexier with age.

"Oh. Good genes, then." We both laugh, though I'm sure it's for different reasons. I'm giddy, unable to contain my joy that Maverick Siciliano is actually flirting with me.

I'm observing him too intensely. I know it, and I'm trying to stop. I just can't help it. "Maybe. I do drink a lot of water, though," he adds in a teasing tone.

"Ah, so your secret is water?" I flirt back.

"Hmm, I suppose it is. Now you know one of my secrets." He moves closer, until his mouth is mere inches from the side of my face. "I think it's your turn to share one of yours," he whispers sensuously, his lips brushing the shell of my ear.

I turn to him, considering. "Well, that depends. What kind of secret are we talking about?" I give him a provocative smile.

Maverick sinks his pearly white teeth into his bottom lip, and my insides turn into mush. "Tell me, Mia. If I wanted to –" I feel his warm lips brush against mine in a kiss that I've dreamed of for so long. It is everything I ever hoped it would be and more.

"Mia, snap out of it. One-D is about to go on," Gabby shouts.

I shake my head, trying to find my way back to reality. Of course, that whole scene was only happening in my mind. Although it felt so real. I could almost taste his lips on mine. I can't help but feel irritated at my cousins for interrupting the glorious fantasy.

"One-D, he-llo, Mia! Did you hear me?" Gabby asks me clearly annoyed.

"Yeah, yeah. Did you say something else?"

"They're about to go on." She tells me with an annoyed expression.

I try to collect myself; I know my parents will want me to be there for this song. I move away from my cousins and join Mom and Dad at their table. They give me a warm smile when I take my seat. "One Thing" is special to them because of the way I used to sing it when I was little. They still talk about it, and I've probably seen the video several hundred times. I guess it's adorable, but I will torture them mercilessly them if they ever show it to anyone outside the family. It's so embarrassing. I may have had a crush on Zane for a hot second, but that was before I heard Maverick sing. Before I bought his first album and saw his perfect, heart-stealing face.

The song is over before I know it and they exit the stage for Dashboard Confessional to come on. They get set up and start performing "Stolen," which is a song my parents say describes their strange yet loving relationship. I glance over to see them cuddling into one another. A few of my brothers make gagging noises as they scramble away from the table, in a hurry to get away from the overt display of affection.

A few months ago, Dad had the family restaurant expanded so a stage could be installed at the front, specifically for their twenty-fifth anniversary party. It feels strange to be watching a private concert so full of fame and talent in the same place we've celebrated every birthday, anniversary, and achievement in our family.

The song ends. The lights go down, the clapping fades, and my heart begins to race. Any moment now, Maverick Siciliano, the sexy Rock-and-Roll God who has starred in all my fantasies since I was old enough to have them, is going to be in the same room as me.

Maverick walks onstage in all his bronzed muscular glory. Chills breakout over my body as he steps up to the microphone. His towers over the audience with his muscular chest and washboard abs on display beneath his tight t-shirt that he's wearing under a black leather jacket. His distressed black jeans hug his thighs in the most delicious way. I bite down on my lip, wondering what he'd look like without any of it on. All kinds of indecent images pop into my brain, and the harder I try to repress them, the hotter I get. I desperately look around the room. I need to think of something else, anything else. I would think looking at my parents would cool my libido, but I feel like he's inside my brain, teasing me, and I can't get him out.

My chest is pounding as the stage lights come back on. They cause a neon sheen to flash over his gorgeous features. The light shines on his slick, jet black hair that is shaved on the sides with a wavy coif styled on top. His soulful almond eyes are filled with sadness as his fingers glide across the guitar strings.

"Only you." Maverick slowly sings the two words, his voice sounding gravelly, tortured, and exhausted. His dreamy eyes scan the crowd, desperately searching for someone. An irrational pain stabs me in the chest as I wonder who he's looking for. He could have brought a girlfriend to see him perform. His dating life has always been so private that I've managed to pretend he didn't have one. I've never been able to understand why I felt such a deep connection with him, but it doesn't change the fact that I do. I scour the room fiercely, following the direction of his eyes. I glance up and his dark gaze meets mine. The air goes thin. My heart begins fluttering wildly, and for a second, I imagine sparks literally flying between us as every hair on my body stands at attention.

I'm intoxicated by how powerful he looks playing his guitar. The way his fingers strum the strings is so erotic. The chords break out so strongly, the room fills with sexual tension.

"I only want you. Oh, only need you. Only you. Oh, only you." Maverick seems to be singing to me, opening his soul to mine. I want to be that person for him so badly, his only one. His performance is so convincing I could easily delude myself into thinking that he wrote the lyrics for me. That I could be his only love.

Maverick's hips roll seductively to the rhythm of the song. I sharply bite down on my lip, drawing blood. *"Consume me. Oh, you consume me. Oh, oh I'm consumed. You've left me wondering. Wondering if you know it."* Every deliciously thick note seems directed at me. I'm seduced into a trance, imagining what it would it be like to be loved by him. To be consumed by his love. How it would feel to have his strong hands all over my body. There are so many things we could do together. Sexy, dirty, naughty things.

"You know it. Yeah, yeah, you know it. Oh, oh, now you know it.Now, now you know it." He gives me a radiant smile and it strikes me like lightning. I need someone to pinch me so I'll know I'm not dreaming. Maverick goes into his guitar solo, and the equipment surrounding him vibrates to the beat. My sex is beating to the same rhythm, my body on fire for him. I'm swaying to the beat, completely lost in our steamy connection.

Maverick leans into the microphone with fevered intensity. *"Only you. Only you. Oh, it's always, only you"* Maverick gives me a sexy wink and I just stare at him in shock.

"Only you. On-ly you.Forever and for always. It's only you." I'm still gaping at him when he winks at me again, adding his signature smile that drives women to throw their underwear at him. I've never understood why women throw their panties onstage at concerts, but right now, it makes perfect sense. Mine are drenched and super uncomfortable.

Maverick has tingles jolting up my spine. It feels like our bodies are calling out to one another. Mine is certainly crying out for him. The moment is sheer perfection. I will always remember it. The song ends and I don't want to look at anything but his face, don't want to break our connection.

That connection is ripped away in a flash when the curtain falls. Maverick is gone. I'm being pulled out of the room by three of my idiot brothers, as I barely contain the urge to scratch their eyes out and run backstage to Maverick.

16

RHYTHM DIVINE
MAVERICK

I'm onstage, about to begin singing my biggest hit for the billionth time. The lyrics start falling from my mouth without thought while I search for a girl I've never seen. When my gaze meets a pair of rich, hazel eyes that shine brighter than the most precious metal, I know I've found Mia. My Mia. She's absolutely stunning with her long, curly brunette hair styled to the side, letting it drape down her bare shoulder. Her tempting plump lips are painted crimson, begging to be kissed.The burgundy dress she is wearing highlights her curves to perfection showing off just a glimpse of the cleavage from her voluptuous breasts. Mia is a seductress who is way too young, too tempting, and way too precious to be starring in my filthiest fantasies. That isn't stopping them from occurring. I know that there are a million reasons why I should nip this in the bud. Then she hits me with her flirtatious smile, sealing her fate to mine. Nothing else matters. I cannot live a life without her in it, cannot stand for her to be with anyone else but me. As I watch her in awe, the romantic lyrics of my song start to feel truly meaningful for the very first time. My heart and soul begin pouring out of me through every word.

Mia has brought out my most basic, animal self. I refuse to let anyone or anything hold me back from making her mine. My passionate serenade turns into a heated, seductive performance. I feel like I'm being pulled inside her soul. She's invaded my brain and my heart. Everyone else in the room disappears. We both get lost in a euphoric rapture.

The song ends and movement next to her makes me break eye contact. I glance at Ignazio and find him looking back and forth between his daughter and me. When he sees me looking at him, he snarls and looks over to the stage manager. He gives a sharp nod, aggressively slicing his hand in front of his throat. The curtain comes down, and my connection with Mia is severed.

I know Ignazio loves his daughter. That he is a ruthless, powerful man who will stop at nothing to keep her from me. But he is in for a rude awakening. I'm going to show him that not even a Mafia King can hold back a Rock-and-Roll God. Not when he's found his eternal muse.

I duck under the curtain, rushing out to the stage. I search frantically, unable to find her in the crowd.

"She's gone," I growl under my breath, furious at my own words. I bite back the howl that attempts to rip its way out of my chest. I've never felt like this before. I can't let her go. Perhaps I should regret my very public seduction. Yet, the only thing I'm regretting is not jumping off the stage and running away with her. Taking her somewhere dark, somewhere private, where I could capture her juicy lips with mine before claiming her fully. My soul was just soaring in her presence, but now in her absence, it has crashed to the ground, shattering into a million pieces.

There is no doubt in my mind. Mia Montagne is the one

for me, pure and simple as that. She will be mine, even if it kills me... which is looking like a real possibility at this point. How ironic that for the first time in a long time, she has made me feel like my life is truly worth living. Without her in my life, I know that I will always feel like there is a gaping hole in my heart.

Several gorilla-sized security guards grab me and escort me outside. I gaze up at the sky as I try to figure out my next step. All I know is that I need to come up with a plan. I look over at Rhett as he runs outside looking for me.

"Hey boss, everything okay? Why did the Montagne security guards kick you out? Did it have something to do with that girl you were staring at the whole time you were performing?"

"The girl I was staring at is Mia Montagne, and I am going to marry her. Can I count on your help?"

Rhett gives me a firm nod, and relief washes over me with the knowledge that I am not alone. We both have a new priority. Together we are going to find a way to get to Mia. I'm dying to see her again. I want to learn everything about her, give her everything and be her everything. There is nothing I wouldn't give to be holding her curvy body against mine and kissing those gorgeous lips. Nothing I wouldn't give to worship her stunning body with mine.

It's been three-and-a-half miserable weeks of emptiness. Rhett and I have been scouring the internet for information on Mia. I've even hired the best private investigator available. We still aren't any closer than when we began. I'm pacing around my living room feeling lost and frustrated. *What if I never see Mia again?* The thought is too devastating to consider.

I've written so many songs about her, but none of them feel like they're good enough. I'm going crazy over trying to create the perfect song to express my feelings. Once it's done and I've found Mia, I'm going to send it to her so that she will know exactly how I feel.

Rhett comes back to our hotel room after surveying the rest of the property. He remains convinced that Ignazio will come for me. I should probably be more concerned about it, but all I care about is being close to Mia. As close as I can be.

"How are you holding up?" he asks with concern as he walks into the kitchen.

"Same old, same old." I brush off his question, unable to tell him the truth. It doesn't seem like a good idea to tell him that I'm losing my ever-loving mind more and more every single day. Every moment I'm without Mia, it feels like another piece of my sanity slips away. I've turned into a maniac who wants to kidnap her. I want to drive her to the nearest church and make it so nobody can ever take her away from me.

"Well, I've got some news," he announces, grabbing the chunky peanut butter out of the pantry and going to grab a spoon.

"Don't tell me you're quitting. Not today. I can't handle it. Seriously." He chuckles before eating a large spoonful of peanut butter.

"Ch-ill." His tongue slaps the roof of his mouth as he attempts to talk. He takes a sip of water before continuing. "Now, don't get too excited. There's a chance, a small chance mind you, but a chance that I have Mia's phone number."

He hands me a slip of paper and everything inside of me focuses on the digits written on it. Suddenly, I feel like there's a chance. A sliver of hope. I attach one of the songs I sung for her to a text message, the best one *I hope*, and hit send, hoping with all my heart that it makes it to Mia.

17
SOS
MIA

The days seem so painfully long now. Each day feels harder and harder to get through. I can't stand having any of the men in my family around me. They all treat me like I'm a little kid with a silly little crush. They don't understand how badly it hurt me that I didn't get to meet Maverick. I didn't get to talk to him. I don't even have a way to reach him.

I doubt my dad or brothers have even noticed the weight I've gained. Fuck you, Ben and Jerry. I thought we were friends. While I'm at it, fuck my dream-crushing family, too.

It's just hopeless. Between my overprotective family and trying to find a way to contact a celebrity, I don't know why I haven't moved on. Not even Google is up to the task. My search history is full of queries that make me look like a deranged stage-five stalker.

I feel my eyes start to tear up again just as my phone's text alert goes off, distracting me from my sad thoughts. I take it out of my pocket and see a message from an unknown number. There's a digital file titled "SOS." I click on it and a song immediately begins playing. As I listen to it, I feel myself smiling as tears trickle down my face.

Mia. Hear my, SOS. Mia. Oh, my Mia. Hear my love.

You had my heart when you smiled my way. Now, it's torn apart. So, torn apart, ever since you went away.

Mia. Hear my, SOS. Mia. Oh, my Mia. Hear my love.

You've got me falling. Oh, I'm falling. Falling, falling, every day. You've got me falling. Oh, I'm falling. Falling, falling in every way.

Mia. Hear my, SOS. Mia. Oh, my Mia. Hear my love.

I've been all around the world. Never, never seeing your equal.

Mia. Hear my, SOS. Mia. Oh, my Mia. Hear my love.

It's you, yeah it's you that I've been missing. It happens, happens all the time. It's got me wishing truly, truly wishing that I could call you all mine.

Mia. Hear my, SOS. Mia. Oh, my Mia. Hear my love.

I can't take it anymore. Maverick wrote and sang this incredibly touching song for me. It came from the depths of his soul and was sung with so much pain in his voice. I have goosebumps all over my body. I'm going out of my mind with the need to see him. I'm just going to have to find a way to sneak out, come hell or high water. I'm pumped with motivation and adrenaline when I remember how Giselle used to break out when she was my age, and no one ever found out.

I send my cousin a text, begging her to share her escape plan with me. I'm going to owe her big time later, but it will be well worth it if this works. I start following her instructions by walking downstairs with some laundry all while playing it cool for the cameras. Once I'm in the laundry room, I put my basket down on the floor. I wait for the camera in here to move in the opposite direction before I go down the laundry shoot head first. While sliding down to the lower level, I squeeze my eyes shut, squealing as I slide down to the lower level. I land on top of a pile of clean towels and scramble to my feet. The cameras will alert our security in seconds. I manage to get out of range before the camera swivels in my direction. I rush outside through the only door that is left unlocked. The door dumped me out into the alley behind the building. I'm hit with the rank smell of trash and I hear feral cats fighting in the near distance. I look around in shock, unable to believe I'm really doing this. My dad will kill me. He will definitely try to kill Maverick. I refuse to let that happen.

I send Maverick a text asking for his address, berating myself for not asking sooner. For all I know, I just snuck out to see him and he could be thousands of miles away. I smile with relief when he sends me an address that is only two blocks away. He asks why but I don't answer. I hope he likes surprises. I wipe my sweaty palms on my pants as I start to walk in his direction.

I glance over at a shop window and see my appearance. I stop, struck with horror. There is no way I am letting him see me like this. I wipe my face with my hands before pulling out my mouth spray and going to town with it. Next, I put on a coat of raspberry lip gloss and roughly brush my thick hair with the small brush I keep in my purse. The last thing I do is spray a little Velvet Orchid perfume on my pulse points, just the way my mom taught me. She always looks so fancy when she does it.

I continue walking, pausing for a deep breath when I see the address that I'm looking for in front of a large brick building. A doorman greets me politely and I smile back as I head toward the reception desk.

"Welcome to the Inn at Henderson's Wharf. It would be my pleasure to help you with whatever you may need this evening." The woman behind the counter is attractive, in a quiet way. Her smile and speech seem very polished, and I get the impression she's been working here a while. I return her kindness with a polite smile of my own.

"I would love to have your help. I've been all around Baltimore looking for my client and..." She leans in with interest. "Can you keep a secret?" I lower my voice to a suspenseful whisper.

"Of course, ma'am. We take our guests' privacy very seriously," she says, her tone serious.

"I knew that I could trust you. See the thing is, my client Maverick Siciliano, is staying in this hotel. I'm sure you know that he is a very famous musician. He is extremely ill. He's so drained, it took him hours to give me proper directions to find him."

"Oh, that sounds awful," she gushes.

"It is. The worst part is that there are media outlets on their way here and if I can't get to him and give him his medicine, they're going to see him looking like the walking dead."

"Oh, my! We must get you up there at once! His fans would be devastated to see him like that." Her deep concern for Maverick is starting to rub me the wrong way. I'm not proud of the jealousy that makes me curl my hands into fists. I know her sweet and helpful nature is just a part of her job. *Probably.* Fine. I admit it, I just don't like seeing another woman worried about him.

I suck it up and give her a sugar-coated smile. "Truly. You're a lifesaver, umm" – I pause, looking at her name badge – "Bridget. You're such a dear. Maverick and I will make sure to let management know how helpful you've been."

"Ah, well thanks, but that isn't necessary. I'm happy to help." Bridget's cheeks flush at the praise as she goes to the private elevator and uses her key card to open it. When the doors slide open, I walk inside and turn around.

"Thank you again, Bridget. I've got it from here. I will have Maverick feeling better in no time," I promise.

"Oh, I do hope so," she calls out just before the doors close completely. I enjoy the short ride up to the fourth floor, which is at the very top of the small but luxuriously decorated inn. The doors ding open, and I see a sign pointing toward his room number. The hallway feels like it's a mile long as I walk to the very last door on the left. Hell, I've waited a lifetime for him, what are a few more minutes? I just hope that I don't let Maverick down. I'm not sure how an inexperienced virgin will please the world's sexiest rock star, but that isn't going to stop me from giving it my all.

18

WE BELONG TOGETHER
MIA

I gulp, growing more anxious with every breath. It takes all my courage, but I finally force myself to knock on his door. Maverick answers the door, looking at me with confusion. "Mia. Mia? Is that really you?" I love the way he says my name. It's still unbelievable to me that he even knows it.

"I had to see you," I admit truthfully, against my better judgment. It's hard to think straight when I'm surrounded by his delicious scent. I feel like I'm floating in a rich cup of espresso doused with creamy dulce de leche sauce. I need to press my lips together to keep myself from drooling.

He ushers me into the hotel room and closes the door behind me, before turning to me and saying, "Mia, I..." He pauses, his dark eyes raking over my face, his expression tender and genuine. "I've wanted you since the first time I heard you speak. I don't know how to explain it. The connection was so powerful, I felt it in my veins. No one has ever made me feel the way that you do. My world has been so empty without you. I missed you so damn much," Maverick admits. I feel like he just took the words right out of my mind. I should be thrilled but a fierce, rotten stubbornness stops me from being happy.

I dig my hands into my hips, glaring at him suspiciously. "You do know who my family is? Who my father is?" I can't let myself get involved with him if he doesn't know what he's getting himself into.

Maverick laughs briefly. "Is there anyone who doesn't?" His jagged voice is so irresistible I want to abandon all rational thought. I can feel my resolve slipping.

"Then you're... you're crazy! You must have a death wish. He *will* kill you." Just considering a world without him in it nearly breaks my heart. I would never let anyone hurt him. I tell myself that while my father may be deadly and he's a man no one would wish to cross when it comes to his children, he would never do anything to hurt me. He knows how I feel about Maverick, even if he doesn't want to admit it.

"Yes... all those things are probably true. But none of it matters. Mia, I've already gone fully insane without you. I will not spend another day wishing for you when I have you right here in front of me." He closes the small gap between our bodies and I feel my body heat up as my heart pounds away inside my chest.

I'm still trying to fight the inevitable. This is serious. I can't just dive in without carefully considering the consequences, without being absolutely certain he considers the consequences. "You don't know what you're saying," I implore, putting my hand on his chest to stop him from kissing me. I need to know that he doesn't have any doubts. I'm not sure I could handle having my heart broken by him. I don't ever want to find out what that would feel like.

Maverick shakes his head, looking so dashing that my breath trips in my throat. "No, Princess... you aren't listening. I'll say it closer to your lips so it registers this time."

"Maverick, I'm ..." I start to whisper breathlessly, not even knowing what I was going to say. He pushes a piece of my hair away from my face as he leans in, his lips skimming over mine.

My eyes widen as he sucks on my bottom lip. "You're mine," he groans possessively, claiming my lips with a steamy kiss. It starts soft, his hands cradling my face gently. I feel light-headed from the emotions rushing through me. Goosebumps break out all over my body.

When our lips finally part, we are both breathing heavily. "Now that I've found you, you're stuck with me," Maverick states, lovingly caressing my cheek.

"Do you really mean that?" I'm tempted to confess how much I love him. But it feels like too much, too fast.

Like he's reading my thoughts, he says, "I love you, Mia." My heart feels like it could burst from hearing the words I so longed to hear. The words I so badly wish to speak aloud myself. I'm dazed. This can't be real. I struggle to believe his simple statement, although I want nothing more than for it to be true.

"You love me?"

"I am so madly in love with you, Mia. You should probably know that I am obsessed with you, really. I will never get enough of you." His face looks worried, like he doesn't know how I will react to his confession, but he shouldn't be. His self-proclaimed obsession settles all my doubts.

"I love you, too! So much!" It feels incredible to say the words. He beams at me and it's as though the sun is shining on me after an interminably long winter.

"Mia. Oh, Mia. Your love means everything to me," Maverick says huskily. His tongue brushes over the seam of my lips, sliding into my mouth as he kisses me with passion. He lifts me up and my thighs belt around his waist as he carries me toward the bed.

Maverick gently lays me down on the mattress, his lustful, smoky eyes wandering over my body. "You drive me wild, Mia," he growls, his strong body covering mine. Our lips connect with heat and urgency.

Maverick's hand moves up my thigh in a heated caress that has my hormones sizzling. "You're not wearing any underwear." He looks at me with a wolfish grin. His fingers graze my sex and I arch into him, moaning.

His thickly calloused fingers slide inside my pussy. "Oh, Princess... you're so wet for me. Let me take care of you."

His fingers feel like magic as they move in and out of me. Each thrust feels better than the last. "Yes. Mmm. Don't stop. Do whatever you want, just please don't stop," I cry, desperately. I have never felt this way before. I feel like I would do anything to make these sensations last forever.

Maverick growls. "Be careful what you say, Princess. My filthy mind will run with your permission to do anything I want to you. You can't even imagine the kinds of explicit things I've fantasized about doing with you."

I unzip my tan moto jacket, slowly teasing him as I reveal my bare breasts for the first time. Maverick hisses like he's in pain and bites down on his fist. "You weren't wearing a bra either." He takes one of my breasts into his wet mouth, feasting on it like a starving beast, sucking on my sensitive nipples as if they're his favorite treat. "I can't get enough. Mmm. One day very soon I'll share these perfect tits with our children. Until then, I'm going to enjoy having them all to myself." His bold statement should shock me, maybe even scare me, but I want to have a family with Maverick more than anything.

"Maverick," I moan with a shudder, drifting to the clouds when his tongue swirls around my pebbled peaks as he teases my clit, strumming it like he does his guitar strings. My core vibrates as my orgasm takes me over the edge. I am completely lost in the pleasure as I scream out his name.

"Mia, come back to me."

"Mmm but... it's so good." I whine, through my blissful state.

"I want you to come again. This time I'm going to get you high off my tongue." Maverick's lips are all over my sex in a flash. It feels so amazing. I want more and more. I'm desperate to feel everything he can do with his hot mouth. He presses his tongue against my pussy. My moans turn to giggles when his beard tickles my thighs.

"Oh, Mia this pretty little pussy tastes so good. So fucking incredible," he groans as his mouth explores my pleasure zones like an expert.

"Maverick... Oh, Maverick! Your mouth is... Oh, that feels so good!"

"Mmm, your cunt tastes so fucking good, Mia. It's so sweet and juicy. I'm so fucking addicted. I'm going to feast on you every night so I can go to sleep with your sweet nectar covering my lips."

Intense pressure builds in my core, bringing me closer and closer to euphoric bliss. "Come for me, Princess," he commands, lighting me on fire. I come completely undone, my cries getting louder as my pleasure escalates.

"Oh, oh, oh, oh, oh," I slip into a dizzy fog as my arousal explodes. My eyes fight to stay open. This day has been incredible, but all the excitement has thoroughly drained me. Maverick pulls me into a hard, passionate kiss before I feel my body go limp and I fall into a deep slumber with a big smile covering my face.

19
MY GIRL
MAVERICK

As I watch my princess sleep peacefully, I debate whether I should rush her to the nearest church or reach out to her parents first. They deserve to know that she's safe. I know it's the right thing to do. However, that doesn't make it any easier. Mia found her way to me; she escaped her father's gilded cage to be with me. I'm keeping her now that I've got her. I will do whatever it takes to keep Mia by my side.

I call Ari to get Ignazio's number, motivated to do the right thing by my girl. "I heard what happened at the concert. You must've felt like absolute shit," he answers, not wasting time with a greeting or small talk.

Even with Mia in my arms, what happened at the party still feels like a fresh wound. "No, Ari. It actually felt really good. I appreciate you mentioning it." I say, sounding more bitter than I intended.

"Chill, kid. Are you having some kind of mental breakdown?" I can't help but chuckle at the irony of this crazy bastard asking me about my mental state.

"What? No. Why are you asking me that?"

"Rumors are spreading through the grapevine. Don't worry, my man, I'll take care of it. I can't have you living in a cuckoo's nest." *Yeah, we can't both live there together.*

"I need Ignazio's number. It's important," I state with an urgent tone, hoping he'll get the message and not go off on any tangents.

"I'll text it to you. But consider this first, snakes slither through the grass, through water... unseen when they attack, if you underestimate them being there." We end the call and I consider his words carefully. With Ari, it's hard to know which pearls of wisdom to discard as drug-induced nonsense and which ones are actually worth heeding.

I take a moment to collect my thoughts before dialing Ignazio's number. Finally, I take a deep breath and hit send.

He answers the phone right away. "Choose your words very carefully," he says, his tone sharp. At first, I'm shocked that he seems to know who's calling, but then I remember who he is. I shouldn't be surprised by anything he does. There are probably no limits to what this man is capable of. And really, it would be far stranger if he weren't already one step ahead of me.

"Mia is safe," I assure him.

"Put her on the phone," he demands.

"It would be better for all of us to talk in person. We can be there shortly."

"That would be wise since your life depends on returning her home safety. Now." He ends the call before I can respond or process how I will handle a face-to-face with the man.

Mia starts wiggling in her sleep, grinding her plump ass against my dick, getting me rock hard. "Fuck," I groan so loudly that she wakes up.

"Maverick, I want you," she whispers, her voice husky

and erotic, provoking my arousal further. Her gorgeous eyes hypnotize me with their brightness.

"We need to wait. We should. We really, really should."

"You don't sound so sure," she purrs seductively. I'm losing my resolve and she can tell. It's probably clear as day that I am dying to claim her, to make her mine forever.

"Mia, you are my princess. You deserve the very best. That is why I'm going to make you mine properly." I kiss her nose gently.

She squishes it adorably with a light giggle. "Mmm, you're mine, too."

"Damn straight, I am. Mia, I want to you have everything you've ever wanted. What is it you want, Princess?"

"You," she states sweetly. I give her my full attention, intent on getting her to tell me more, even though her initial answer fills me with pride. "I enjoy making logos for businesses. I've made a few for my family. I'd like to learn more about graphic design, and maybe marketing."

"I'd love to learn more about it too. Would you share that with me? We could learn together."

"I would love that! I want to share everything with you," she says with a suggestive wink.

"Oh, Mia...you're killing me baby." I try to compose myself but it's damn hard. Literally. So damn hard.

"My age doesn't bother you?" I get scared when she doesn't say anything at first, but before I can think of anything to say to reassure her, she answers.

"No. I love how mature you are. You're so intelligent. You've experienced so much. You've been around to see a lot of historical things happening. " She teases me flirtatiously. I shut her sassy mouth up with a deep kiss.

"I'm going to give you everything. We just need to start things the right way. That's why we need to go see your parents. I just spoke with your dad and he is expecting us."

"That sounds awful. Can't we just run away?" I laugh, wishing it could be that simple.

I swat her bottom as I get out of bed, needing to get away from the temptation she presents before I get carried away and her father murders me. "I am not running away. You're mine. It's time for your family to see that."

It takes about twenty minutes for us to get to her place, but it feels like I barely took a breath before I'm parking my car. We take the elevator to the first floor where we are immediately greeted by the worried faces of her parents.

"I can't believe you actually showed up!" Ignazio shouts, enraged. I can't blame him, though. This really isn't a favorable position for me to be in. Stella is standing beside him, but Ignazio has my full attention.

"I didn't have to bring her back. We could be at a chapel right now." I snap my mouth shut, unable to believe I was stupid and insane enough to say that to him. My love for Mia makes me bold, it fills me with the will to fight for her. I look him straight in the eye, unwilling to budge an inch.

"You've got a lot of nerve. I'll give you that," he growls aggressively, starting to take a step toward me. Stella grabs his arm and moves into him, pressing her body against him. His body relaxes slightly, but his face remains menacing.

"Dad, please hear us out," Mia requests, her tone pleading. It appears to appeal to his softer side. A side I wasn't sure existed. A side that I am certain few others have seen.

"I'm here out of respect. I have a lot of respect for you and your family," I tell him, speaking from the heart.

"Ha! Respect! You fucking call this respect?" he yells,

waving his hand angrily. "What's your angle here?" He studies my face suspiciously.

"I don't have an angle, sir. I am in love with your daughter. I love Mia with everything inside of me. I would do anything for her. I know you understand the lengths a person will go to for their soul mate. *That* is why I brought her back. She loves her family and I refuse to stand in the way of that. Not when I know how unhappy it would make her. That and, I wanted you to see for yourselves that she wasn't in any danger."

"Thank you for that. We were so worried." Stella breaks a bit of the tension with her soft words and even softer smile. The reprieve doesn't last long.

"None of that changes the fact that Mia is only eighteen years old. You are not going to come into my home and rob the cradle!" Ignazio roars, sounding even angrier than before.

Mia's hands ball into tight fists as her cheeks turn crimson with rage. "Cradle! Cradle? Seriously? I have had it. I am not a little kid anymore! Hell, you all drive me so crazy around here, I'll be getting gray hairs any day now," she screams at the top of her lungs. Her father, a man I know to be a hardened criminal, looks devastated by her outburst. It's clear that no matter what this man has done, he loves his family more than anything else in the world.

He drops his chin to his chest. "I told you. I did, Stella. She's doing it. Breaking it. My heart. I knew this was going to happen one day," he says in a choked whisper, speaking to his wife. The emotion in his voice tugs at my heart.

"Come on, now. Mia is an adult, Ignazio. You know that. It's time we starting treating her like one."

"No way! I think it's time for him to leave." *Not a chance in hell.*

"I'm not going anywhere without, Mia," I respond

bravely, ready to show him how far I will go for the love of my life. It felt like I lost her once already, and that was before I even knew her. I couldn't survive that a second time. Especially not now that I know how perfect she feels in my arms.

"Dad! I love Maverick! Why can't you see that?" Mia asks beseechingly.

"I'm trying to, sweet pea," he answers softly, and I can tell it wasn't easy for him to admit.

"Try harder!" she demands, her eyes heated with ferocity. I'm beyond impressed and uncomfortably turned on. Her willingness to take on her father, an infamous criminal, has me desperately wishing we were alone. I cannot wait to show her how much I worship her.

"In that case, he isn't going anywhere," Ignazio states firmly. My jaw drops. I certainly wasn't expecting that. What the hell do I do now?

"What? No! Dad!" she huffs, her hands fisting on her hips. "Mom! Please say something," Mia pleads.

"Those are my conditions, Mia. Not even your mother can change my mind on this. If Maverick really wants to be with you, he will live here. *After* you are married." My jaw drops to the floor. My ears must be deceiving me. There is no way I heard him say that he is going to allow Mia to marry me. It fully hits me for the first time. I've received dozens of awards and accolades, and for a long time, I thought that was enough. But nothing could have prepared me for this. Nothing could be more fulfilling than being Mia's husband.

"Oh, Daddy! Thank you! Thank you so much!" Mia squeals, running into her dad's arms and giving him a huge hug. She kisses his cheeks multiple times, earning her a charming smile from her father. The same smile he passed down to his daughter. The same smile I hope to see on my own child's face very soon. Thinking about our future makes me grin. I can't wait to get started on making our family.

"Remember, I loved you first, sweet pea." He holds her closely and Stella sighs, watching them with so much love shining in her eyes. I also sigh, but with the relief of knowing that everything is going to be okay now.

"I will. I Promise." I can see how strong their bond is. I want to have that with our children, though I am certain they will love their mother more. They'd be crazy not to.

Mia goes to her mom and gives her a hug before coming to stand by me.

"I'll be back really soon, Princess. I'm going to go get a ring and a priest and be back here as soon as I can. Before you have a chance to change your mind." The last sentence I direct at Ignazio. His eyebrows shoot up, and he almost looks impressed by my boldness. I give my princess a kiss on the cheek, choosing not to push things by kissing her on the lips in front of her father. Then I leave, fiercely motivated by the idea of being able to call Mia my wife by the end of the night.

On my way to the nearest jewelry store, I think about how I wasn't ever truly content being single. It just seemed like the safest route to protect myself from getting used and hurt. Loneliness almost began to feel normal. But Mia has made me realize how lonely I really was, and I can hardly contain the joy I feel at knowing I will never feel that way again. I've been all over the world and know that there is nobody out there quite like her. There is no one out there who is more perfect for me. While I look around for a ring fit for my princess, I put in another call to Ari.

He answers on the fifth ring, just like always. "Mav, bro it's been a long time since I've heard from you," he quips.

"Yeah, yeah, yeah. I need another favor."

"Whoa, whoa, whoa, I just got up from a nap. Give me a second." He yawns and I hear a lighter spark. He inhales and lets out a long breath. "I had a dream about you. In my dream, I was a dinosaur running through a dust storm. And then I evolved into the moon, swimming into the sky. Then I started to glow, turning bright, and became the sun." I have no idea what the hell he's talking about... and I'm not entirely sure I want to.

"Wow ... Ari, you really should probably be more careful about what you put into your body."

"Mav, it was a sign. The moon and the sun. I was both the moon and the sun. Which means big things are about to happen. Big, big things, kid."

"You're right Ari, big things are happening. That is why I need you to help me out. Can you get a priest over to Ignazio's tonight?"

"Consider it done, kid. I sure hope you guys have a happy life together."

"Thank you, Ari!" I'd tell him I owe him one, but he's the kind of person who collects with a huge interest rate.

"You need to relax more. I'm going to send you something to help. It's a delightful chamomile, tea tree blend. It will cleanse you. Trust me, it will get you ready for new beginnings."

"Thanks, Ari, that is very thoughtful of you." I won't be drinking the tea when it arrives. I've had one of his "teas" before. The next day, I found myself halfway across the country waking up on top of the Hollywood sign, my head feeling like it was going to explode from pain. Besides I don't need a tea or anything else to feel high. I have Mia. She is my personal addiction.

A princess-cut ruby ring with a vine wreath of marquis diamonds surrounding it catches my eye. As soon as I see it,

I know. That is the ring I will be putting on Mia's finger. I really hope she loves it because she's going to be wearing it for the rest of her life.

20
HEROES(WE COULD BE)
MIA/MAVERICK

I'm getting married to Maverick Siciliano. I've repeated it in my head dozens of times, and still, it feels like an impossible dream. He hasn't been gone long but I already can't wait for him to return. It doesn't help that my goofball brothers are testing my sanity.

"We should get a tiger for protection. No one messes with you when the king of the jungle is around," Cruze suggests, breaking the thick tension in the room.

"Tigers aren't the king of the jungle, you moron. Lions are," Roque tells him with a punch to his arm.

"Yeah well, I might be a moron but at least I know how to dress myself. I'd be lying if I said I liked your outfit. Are you getting ready to go to *The Matrix*?" The humor is lost on Roque. Cruze really should know better, he's only going to provoke Roque's temper.

I'm sure any second now Cruze is going to be laid out on the floor. "What's wrong with what I'm wearing?" Roque's fists clench as he studies his outfit, and I laugh out loud when I see what Cruze is talking about. Roque is wearing sunglasses that look just like the ones Lawrence

Fishburne wore, making *The Matrix* comparison spot-on. All he's missing is the leather trench coat.

"It's tacky and... well, I hate it," Cruze half jokes. I'm sure he does hate it. Sometimes, I need to remind myself that even my brothers have high fashion in their blood. It just looks like Roque woke up missing his God-given fashion sense this morning.

Stefano walks in, eating a green apple with an amused grin. "Hey Cruze, I thought you'd still be locked in the dumpster Roque put you in," he chuckles.

Cruze glares at us when we all start laughing. "Yeah. Well, I got out," he shouts. We laugh even harder.

"I'm going to bed. I despise all your faces... so much." Cruze huffs loudly as he makes his dramatic exit.

"You're dead to me." Roque calls out to him, and Cruze whips back around and gives him the middle finger.

"Enough! I am *not* amused," Dad roars. "Go to your rooms, both of you." They leave slowly, pausing at the doorway, probably hoping that Dad will start lecturing me. They finally give up, disappointed, when they realize nothing is going to happen.

The weird silence is back. It's uncomfortable. Unable to take it anymore, I get up and go to my room to get ready. When I get there, my phone dings with a text from Maverick. Apparently the priest is on his way over right now and Maverick will be headed back soon. I laugh giddily as I go to take a shower. I cannot believe I'm going to be married to the man of my dreams in just a few hours!

Everything happens in a blur once Maverick gets back. My parents watch us sign our wedding certificate, and the exhausted priest leaves minutes later. My mom pulls Dad away when he starts glaring daggers at Maverick. Suddenly, I'm alone in my condo with Maverick. My husband.

Maverick is my husband! This is *our* condo now. I feel my body begin to heat as I realize what happens next.

MAVERICK

This is the start of something great. I can feel it deep in my bones. Seeing my name next to hers on the marriage certificate was the greatest moment of my life so far.

Now I am in Mia's sanctuary and all I notice is the color scheme, which is dark green with gold accents. I'm too preoccupied with thoughts of claiming her, of making her mine, to pay any more attention to my surroundings. The anticipation has built to a crescendo. My balls have never ached so hard for so long. Mia is the only one who can take the edge off. There's an inferno building inside of me, threatening to burst if I don't get to see her naked soon, if I have to wait much longer to feel her silky, golden skin against mine as I sink inside of her.

"I can't believe we are married." Mia is gazing down at her ring, her eyes full of wonder and a dreamy smile on her face. It's obvious she loves her ring with how often I've noticed her staring at it.

"You better believe it. You're all mine, now." I vow, sealing my promise with a kiss. Mia is imprinted on my soul. I feel so fortunate to call her mine, to know we will build a family together. I'm breathing hard, raring to get started. I was running around town most of the day, and even though the thought of being away from her for even a moment kills me, I really need to shower first. I go into her bathroom and wash as quickly as possible, barely getting all the soap off before I'm out of the shower and wrapping a towel around my waist.

My control snaps when I step out of the bathroom and

see the lust-filled expression on my sweet, innocent wife's face.

21

WILD LOVE
MIA/MAVERICK

Maverick is in the shower, and ever since he went into the bathroom and shut the door, my curious mind has been conjuring all sorts of dirty things. He finally walks out, wearing nothing but a thin towel clinging to his hips, doing little to hide his hard body. And boy is it hard. Everywhere. His chest is muscular and well-defined, and his abs are sculpted beyond perfection. My pulse begins to race. I bite my lip as I gawk at his glistening muscles, my eyes tracing the path of the water droplets sliding under the towel. I feel like I can barely catch my breath when my eyes get stuck on his erection under the towel. It looks large and intriguing. I want it.

"What are you thinking about, Mia?" he asks, his voice low and gravelly. I lick my lips and he groans. I see his big cock twitch under the towel.

"I-I'm so sorry. I, uh, I shouldn't be staring," I stammer, blushing.

"You want something to lick?" I feel my sex clench at his words and the sexy tone he used. I do want something to lick. I want to know what it's like to lick him. Want to see how he will react and know what he tastes like. *Can he tell what I'm thinking?* "Come here," he commands, and I step forward, taking a deep, nervous breath.

Maverick drops his towel and stands before me naked, letting me see all of him. It's the first time I've seen a fully naked man in person. My legs are shaking from nerves. He's *huge.*

"I want to feel those sexy lips around my cock."

I rub my legs together. This is complicated. My lust-filled brain is screaming at me to give him what he wants, but I'm terrified. I've never done this before. What if I'm bad at it?

Maverick begins stroking his length, watching me with hungry eyes. I feel a spurt of jealousy, wanting to be the one to give him pleasure. My fear turns to annoyance, and I drop to my knees and look up at him, hoping he will give me some guidance. My stomach clenches with arousal when his gaze meets mine and he rubs the tip of his cock along the seam of my lips.

"You look so fucking sexy on your knees. Open up for me, Princess." I lick around the head of his cock, maintaining eye contact the whole time. "I love watching you lick me. It's so hot." I open my mouth wider and take him deeper into my mouth.

"Suck it. Just like that, Princess. Fuck," Maverick groans, his eyes locked on his length disappearing into my mouth. He grits his teeth as he wraps my hair around his strong fist and starts thrusting his thickness between my lips, stretching my jaw as far as it can go. "You're doing such a good job. So damn good, baby," he praises hoarsely. I moan around him, his words flooding me with desire. I work him in and out of my mouth, taking him as far as I can, eagerly trying to take more and more every time. I want to make him feel pleasure like he's never known before. I want him to love what I can do for him so much that he craves it. Begs me for it. He thrusts harder, pushing into my throat. He holds me there, groaning deeply as my eyes water. I taste his salty pre-cum on my tongue. I feel slightly dizzy from the lack of air, and I'm shocked to find out how much I love it.

Maverick gives me a sly grin. "I'm going to come inside this hot little mouth of yours." I moan, his words making me even hotter.

"Mia," Maverick groans wildly. The desperate urgency in his voice and the deep longing in his eyes makes me feel sexy and desirable. He's watching me hungrily, on the edge of losing control. Our moans come together in an erotic chorus. I suck him harder, deeper, until he explodes in my mouth.

"Mmm, this mouth is officially mine. I'm going to spend the rest of the night laying claim to everything else that belongs to me."

MAVERICK

She stands up and I turn her around, pulling her back into my chest. Her breasts are so full and round I can't keep my hands from massaging them. Her sultry moans are driving me insane. I need more of those sweet sounds. More of her.

All of her, for the rest of my life.

I run my thumbs over her pert nipples, groaning. "Mmm, Princess, your perfect tits are driving me wild. I'm dying to put my mouth all over them." My desire for her grows more intense, knowing I have her right where I want her. Mia is tied to me from this day on.

"Should I… um. Should I take my dress off? Do you want me to? I'm sorry. I've never done this before, Maverick. I-I'm a virgin." My dick jumps at her words. At the knowledge that I am the only man who will ever see her this way. I cannot wait to claim my sweet innocent virgin's cherry. Mia was always meant to be mine.

"I want to see every inch of you, Princess. Take off the dress."

"I want you to see me too," she whispers shyly, turning around. I am going to feast on her body, going to mark her golden skin as mine.

She takes off her dress, showing me her white lace bra and panty set. I growl. My eyes greedily devour her exposed flesh and I pull her closer, closing my eyes and relishing the sensation of her body against mine. I'm so hot for my princess. I move toward the bed and fall onto the mattress, pulling her with me and rolling on top of her. My need to explore her gorgeous body is driving my every action.

I slide my hand under her back and unclasp her bra, sliding it down her arms and baring her breasts to my ravenous gaze. I sit back on my knees, gently grazing her nipples with the tips of my fingers. "Oh, Maverick. I love it when you touch me there," Mia moans seductively. My erection grows impossibly hard at her words. I love that I am capable of giving her so much pleasure.

My tongue replaces my fingers, flicking back and forth over one nipple, then the next. I need more. With a growl, I begin nipping and sucking every inch of her ample breasts, her body writhing beneath me.

"Yes! Oh, yes!" she screams.

"Mia, you have no idea how long I've waited for you. I'm always going to take care of you. Always." I need Mia to know that I'm going to protect her while I show her body the kind of pleasure no one else can give her.

In a flash, I'm off the bed, yanking her toward me. I tug her panties down roughly, leaving them at mid-thigh, impatient to touch her. To feel her wet heat. I claim fierce ownership of her sweet little pussy by cupping it in my hand as Mia wiggles her legs, trying to get her panties off. I grab her hip with my other hand, stilling her movements. My eyes lock with hers and I hiss, "Mine!" I need her to recognize that she belongs to me. Every part of her.

She nods earnestly. Reassured, I finally look down and watch as I skim my fingers over her folds. She squirms as I make broad circles around her clit, getting closer and closer. Finally, I reach my target and press down hard. Mia's back arches off the bed, her mouth open in a silent scream. I caress her button gently until she relaxes with a moan. "Oh, oh ... I love it when you touch me there, too."

She stops breathing for a second when I push a finger inside her tight channel. She grips me tight, and I groan, feeling the inside of her tight pussy for the first time.

"Is this too much?" I ask, searching her face for any sign of pain. I can't bear the idea of hurting her, not even in the throes of passion.

Mia eagerly grinds her slick pussy against my hand. "No, no ... please don't stop."

"I won't, Princess. I won't. My girl doesn't need to beg. You're too special for that. Do you understand?" I want her to know that I will always give her anything she wants. She doesn't even need to ask.

She beams at me with a look of adoration that leaves me dizzy. "Maverick, I want you. I need, I need to be with you."

"I know, baby. I know what you need. I need it too. But first, I need to get my princess ready." I continue to work my fingers in and out of her snug walls, stretching her as her sweet juices run down my hand. "Fuck, Princess ... you're so damn tight. You're going to destroy me." I slip my fingers out of her warm pussy, moaning as I lick her sweet cream from my hand.

Desire is running rampant through my body. I grip my

throbbing cock in my hand and gently slap her glistening sex with it. "Does this belong to me?"

"Yes. Yes!" she cries.

"Good girl," I growl. "Keep those sexy legs spread nice and wide for me."

I run the tip of my cock through her slick folds a few times before I push inside of her virgin heat. My eyes roll into the back of my head as Mia's pussy ruins me in the best way imaginable. Mia's wet heat is wrapped around me so tightly I can't think straight.

"Maverick, oh Maverick. It hurts ... so good. So, so good but ahhh it- it kind of stings too. It feels so big." I slow down, giving her time to adjust.

"You're doing so good. Try to relax for me, princess. It will feel better soon."

"It does. Oh, it does. I want more. I want to feel all of you." I push in the rest of the way, giving her all ten inches of my thick length.

"Oh, fuck! You're taking me so deep, Princess." I grasp her thick black hair in my hands, gripping her head tighter as I thrust inside her slowly and deliberately.

"Maverick," she gasps. "Oh, Maverick ... I feel it coming."

I speed up, burying myself inside of her and sliding nearly all the way out. I pound my dick into her harder. "Come for me, Princess," I command gruffly. Her body unravels for me as her moans turn to soft whimpers.

I feel her spasming around me and my own orgasm hits me. I freeze, buried deep inside of her and filling her with my seed. Purposefully driven to take root in her womb. I stare down at her for a moment, entranced. My wife is the most gorgeous woman on the planet, no comparison. It's more than her just being gorgeous or the intense sexual attraction we share. She has a magnetic energy so powerful

I could feel it onstage, pulling my soul into the audience. Seeing her precious face up close while we made love was an experience I plan to repeat every single day for the rest of my life.

My orgasm is so vivid, it's like death, like a rebirth. It's everything, and it has turned me into a possessive, depraved version of myself. "You're mine, Princess. Mine and mine alone." I growl, tugging her hair so I can claim her lips with a wild, passionate kiss. We can't get enough of each other. I know I will never get enough of my wife. My obsession for my muse is eternal. Mia is everything that I've ever wanted, and so much more. She has brought harmony back into my life by agreeing to be mine. I plan to spend my life satisfying her needs until she is utterly and completely spoiled.

"We're going to grow old together," I promise, as she's drifting off to sleep. She gives me her priceless smile as she melts into me. I could write a million songs about Mia's smile. And that is just what I plan to do.

22

ISN'T SHE LOVELY
MAVERICK

EIGHT YEARS LATER...

Madeline walks slowly toward the front of the stage and grabs the mic, looking at me with fear in her eyes. I'm just as nervous as she is, but I'm doing my absolute best to hide it. I can see her bottom lip begin to quiver, and Mia tenses up by my side. She squeezes my hand tightly as we smile at our brave girl.

I give my adorable little angel the proudest smile I can muster. I hope she can sense our support up there. I hope she can see in my eyes that I've got her back. I hope she knows that I always will. She pauses, squeezing her eyes shut and taking a deep breath. Then she opens them and begins to sing.

I see the switch flip inside of her. I swear, a star was just born. Her voice goes from smooth and sweet to raspy and powerful. Before she even finishes the last note, everyone in the crowd is on their feet, cheering. I have never been so proud. I'm blown away by her talent.

I admit, I might be biased, but after spending the majority of my life in the music industry, I know true talent when I see it. My little angel ends her performance by dropping into a curtsy then spinning around in her frilly, turquoise dress. It's probably the cutest thing I've ever seen.

Her biggest fan, her grandfather, is cheering the loudest. "Bravo! Bravo, Madeline! Bravo! That's my grand baby!" Ignazio shouts, looking at all the people around him with a proud grin, making sure everyone knows his relationship to the beautiful little girl who just blew them away, before kissing his smiling wife on the cheek.

Madeline's Aunt Chloé whistles with her fingers while her Uncle Stefano cheers enthusiastically next to her. Everyone laughs when Mia's brothers rush the stage, wrapping their niece in their embrace. Roque lifts Madeline above his head, seating her on his shoulders and carrying her off the stage and into the crowd. She's laughing as she hands out high fives and collects bouquets of flowers from her family and fans. I have never been so full of pride ... or fear. My girl is going places and this family *really* doesn't need any more fame.

23
CELEBRATION
MIA

"Thank you all for joining us tonight to celebrate twenty-five years of love," Maverick's best friend Rhett starts his speech as he stands on stage next to his manager. Ari is currently distracted by the ceiling and smiling at it. "Salute, to the best couple I know." Rhett raises his glass. "Salute!" Everyone shouts with their glasses held high.

"Congrats, kid. You still owe me some favors for making this all happen."

"I'm still scared for the day that you finally call it in," My husband jokes half-heartedly knowing he should be slightly concerned. The last one of these little favors involved us pet sitting an albino python for a month.

"Mav, you should share your story. Let its narrative fly into our minds." Ari implores to me passionately, thinking that he is talking to Maverick.

We hide our giggles as he smiles at me in recollection. "I was getting ready to perform at her parents' anniversary party. Before I went on, I was standing in the hallway when I heard the most alluring voice. It spoke to my soul. When I saw her for the first time, I was standing onstage, and I thought to myself, I am going to marry that girl. I had a ring on her finger the same day I kissed her for the first time. We got married that night, right here in the home we all still live in. It has been over thirty years and we are still." Maverick chuckles when I squeeze his arm as I look up at him with tear-filled eyes. He always gets me so emotional when he tells our story.

"It gives me chills every time. I still can't believe how we met. I thought I was in love with him before I ever knew him but falling in love with him was better than even my wildest dreams. It happened right away. Our connection was so strong that everyone could see it, before we ever even spoke to one another. My dad rushed me out of the room and forbade me from seeing him. I didn't have any way to contact Maverick. I thought the pain of it would kill me. He didn't forget about me, though." I give my husband a loving smile.

"There was no way I could have. Her face was burned into my memory the second I saw it. Her dad didn't like me one bit, though, and I knew it. It took a while for me to find a way to contact her. Took a whole lot longer to win him over. He enjoyed making me work for my spot in the family." Thinking about it brings a smile to my face. My husband fought hard for our family. And it was worth every second. "Eventually I wore him down, along with her mob of brothers who all threatened to kick my ass six ways to Sunday."

"Dad has always liked your music ... and that you're Italian," I joke with a warm smile. Maverick belonged in my family. They all adore him now. My brothers even wrestle with him, proof that he is one of them.

"Now that he likes me, he loves that I'm Sicilian," I chuckle lightly at the memory of how happy he was when he found out his granddaughter would be able to trace her roots back to Italy on both sides of her family tree. My dad is happiest when our family is enjoying a traditional Italian feast together. We catch up with each other and on occasion dad brings in Opera singers for entertainment.

"It guts me to think of how things could have gone very differently. I am so fortunate that my wife was as committed to our future as I was and that she fought for our love. Blessed that she knew her father would come around because of his all-consuming love for his children and his desire to see them happy. And thankful for the way she conned her way up to my hotel room to surprise me. Best surprise of my life. I knew we were meant to be together. Just like you know the night when it's dark."

"I was so worried you wouldn't want to get married or commit to one person. You could have had anyone. You could have had your pick of so many different women."

"There is only one you, Mia. I thought you would be the one to find someone better. Every time I close my eyes, I thank the universe that you're mine. It's so hard to believe that a princess fell for a musician. I am so lucky I found you."

"I am too."

"I even got her to marry me twice." Everyone laughs.

"It also made my mom very happy that we could plan the celebration together." Maverick brings my hand to his lips, planting a tender kiss on my palm. It reminds me of when we had our first dance as man and wife, and he did the same thing. "Our second wedding was pretty epic."

"It really was the most incredible wedding. And not just because she was reinforcing the fact that she was mine," Maverick laughs to our guests who join in.. Everyone knows how much he loves hearing me tell him that I belong to me.

"We had a huge traditional Sicilian cassata cake. All our

guests were so impressed by it." I recall it being delicious as well.

"It was massive! The size of a Christmas tree. It had over twenty layers, with candied fruit shaped into flowers all over it."

"Right. Well, he couldn't have cared less about the cake. He couldn't wait until we could leave," I joke to my husband.

"Naturally. I always want my, Princess all to myself."

"That's how I feel in love with a rock star," I joke, concluding our speech to wrap the evening up faster. Maverick has that stormy look in his eyes that gets me hot all over. It never fails to make my knees weak. "Let's sneak out." I whisper seductively.

Maverick's face lights up with excitement. "I love you, Princess, always."

AMOUR NOIR

Chloé: I'm a long way from home, but I'm grateful to have left my life in France behind me. Being a Mafia Princess brought me nothing but misery. The paparazzi in the states don't know or care who I am. But there's Stefano. Stefano wants to know everything about me, but I can't let him find out who I really am. If he finds out who I am or discovers the even bigger secret I'm keeping from him, everything will be ruined.

Stefano: I'm going to throttle my sister. I'm headed to Amour Noir to find out what the hell she was thinking, setting me up on a blind date with that obnoxious woman. I'm all fury when I walk inside, my face a formidable mask of rage. I pause when I see the most delectable treat sipping from a fluted glass. When I step into the light, I see the frightened expression in her eyes. She lets out a gasp of alarm, spraying champagne all over me. Her fear turns to shock when my tongue darts out of my mouth, licking the champagne from my lips slowly, sensuously, and I wonder what my future wife tastes like.

24
ONE-CHLOÉ

I'm so grateful that my father called in a favor with his good friend Mr. Montagne so I could get away from my very hectic, ridiculously public life. I couldn't go anywhere without a camera in my face. I've lived a lifetime of it, and I finally had enough. This new freedom is even more liberating than I thought it would be. I bet I could even walk down the street picking a wedgie without anyone paying me the least bit of attention.

"I'll be the perfect guest, Mom. Yes, everything seems perfectly safe. I'll call you when I get off work. Yes. I'm walking in now." I put my hand over the receiver when I see Mademoiselle Montagne smiling at me.

"Good morning, Chloé!" I wave at my new boss, whose positive energy is already making me feel less nervous about the first day of my new life.

"Bonjour, Mademoiselle. My mom would like to speak with you. If that is alright?"

"Of course, and please, call me Stella, dear." She smiles at me warmly, reaching for my phone. I hand it over, trying to hide my face so she can't see how embarrassed I am. My skin is so pale, I've never been able to hide my feelings. My entire body flushes red anytime I experience strong emotions about anything.

"Bonjour, Charlotte. Oh, don't you worry, we will take care of her, just like she's one of our own. Yes, of course. You know Ignazio, we have more security than the President. Of course, I will let you know right away if anything does happen. But it won't. Sure, I'll tell her. Au revoir." She ends the call and hands my phone back with a smile.

"Sorry," I whisper shyly.

"Oh, honey. If you think your mom is bad, you should talk to my children. Even my 28 year old is still my baby." She chuckles as she changes the sign on the door to open. I try to keep my jaw from hitting the floor. I have no idea how this gorgeous woman is old enough to have a son in his late twenties. "If my son doesn't call me at least once a day, he knows I'll start checking hospitals. If he isn't in one and doesn't have a really good explanation for not checking in, my husband would probably send him to one just for making me worry." She turns around and gestures for me to follow her to the back of the store.

"Oh...wow."

"I'm only joking, honey. Well, I hope so anyway. We've never had to find out. Stefano is very good at putting up with my harassment and occasional stalking." She lets out a tinkling laugh, her expression laced with amusement at my startled reaction.

"My mom told me you have a large family," I mention, hoping she'll tell me more about them. I'm an only child and this is a big change for me. I want to try to be prepared so I don't act like a complete weirdo.

"I do, and we are all very close. I know you aren't used to big families, but you will love them all, I promise. They're crazier than aye-ayes but it's a good brand of crazy. You'll never be bored; I can assure you of that much." She lets out a fake evil laugh, and I can't help but chuckle.

I'm so relieved to find she is so friendly and welcoming. Although, there do seem to be some language barriers. "Aye-ayes? I don't know this word."

"They're a rare breed of lemurs with the most haunting eyes." She reveals in a comical, spooky whisper.

I look them up on my phone and she isn't wrong. The one I'm looking at almost looks like a bat, with a frizzy nest for hair, large elfish ears, long witchy fingers, and it has bulging yellow eyes. I'm going to have a hard time getting the image of those eyes out of my head when I'm trying to sleep tonight. They are oddly adorable, though.

"Let's fold some shirts, and when my daughter comes in, I will show you how to use the register. We usually do a light lunch here and then have a long family dinner around eight."

"That sounds great. I don't eat much." I regret my words as soon as they leave my lips. I have no clue why I said that. It isn't at all true. I just don't eat much around people. I was once photographed with a piece of kale hanging over my lip, and I've been wary of eating in public or in large groups of people ever since.

"Oh, well that's about to change. Large Italian families means there are copious amounts of food. At all times. We won't be happy until you're full to bursting." We share a laugh as we go into the back room, which is filled with boxes and clothing racks.

"Sounds like a good change. Italian food is my favorite."

After about an hour spent folding clothes and straightening up the displays, I hear the bell over the door jingle and look over as a beautiful petite woman comes in, a powerful aura surrounding her. She walks with a swagger full of confidence, and I find myself envying her for it. I was already psyched to meet someone my age, and now I'm even more so. She looks intriguing. I'm so used to stuffy, boring people. The blue tint in her black hair makes her seem even bolder, and I feel like we are going to have a lot of fun together. Although there's a good chance she's on lockdown, the same way I was at home. I've heard her brothers and father are super overprotective. But she seems like the kind of person who knows how to work her way around the rules and get away with it.

She shakes her head in an odd way when she sees me. She looks at her mother with a bewildered expression. Considering the fact that I'm the daughter of one of the most powerful Corsican mafia bosses in Marseille, you'd think I would be able to hold my own. The truth is, I am nothing like my parents. I'm only twenty-one, and there are so many things I've never done, it would take less time to list the things I *have* done. But I have dealt with my fair share of judgment. Private school with mean girls meant being called evil, disgusting, and immoral, all while trying to keep away from the lens of the paparazzi. That was my hell, and I will never go back to living that way.

"Stop being rude, Electra! Come meet Chloé."

"Sorry... sorry. Nice to meet you! I'm Electra. I know I'm acting like a total spaz. It's just that when I saw you, I realized something." I raise my brow, waiting for her to continue. She starts laughing, casually walking behind the register. I wait impatiently for her to continue as she grabs a metal drawer from under the counter.

My curiosity is killing me, and I can't wait any longer. "So...are you going to tell me what you realized?" She looks up with wide eyes, like she doesn't know what I'm talking about. She shakes her head as she pulls a set of keys out of her purse.

"Oh, no. I can't tell you. It's just someone is going to be

pretty upset with me later. A madman." She explains cryptically.

"A madman?" I question, wanting her to tell me more. I've always been too curious for my own good, but not knowing things makes me feel like I'm going to burst.

"Mhmm. Aren't they all, though?" She laughs and I hesitantly join her, unsure how to respond.

"Luckily, I'm the baby of the family so he knows I'm untouchable." My lips purse as I try to figure out who she's talking about. It really seems like she isn't going to elaborate any further and my suspicions are confirmed when she says, "Come on, I'll show you how to open. Later we can pop some champs to celebrate your first day in B-More." Yup, she's definitely not going to tell me. That's fine. I'll figure it out eventually, and I'll have fun doing it with some champagne in my system.

"That sounds lovely. It's very important to stay hydrated," I joke, causing us both to burst out laughing so loudly, we gain Stella's attention. She doesn't get upset at my unprofessional behavior. Instead, she smiles, like she's happy we're getting along so well.

"You're fantastic, Chloé. We are going to get along famously. Just like sisters."

25
TWO-STEFANO

I'm so confused right now. Is my sister messing with me? She can't seriously think I would have anything in common with this vapid money grubber sitting across me. I'm beyond annoyed at this point. This strange woman has mentioned her credit card bills and shopping addiction, pretending like she's joking, more than once. I've run out of small talk and my promise to be polite has worn thin.

"*The Godfather* is my favorite movie. I... just... *love* a powerful man with a gun." She purrs seductively. Okay, that's it. I'm out of here.

"Look, I'm going to cut to the chase. I don't want to waste each other's time here. This isn't going to work. I'm not interested, and I am a very busy man."

"Mmm, even busy men need to relax sometimes, don't they?" she asks in a husky tone as she reaches her hand across the table to grab mine, but I pull back before she can touch me. "Come back to my place and I can show you all kinds of things that will interest you."

I want to reply, 'Too bad I'm not interested in the circus,' but I manage to refrain. I'm trying not to be such a prick this year. It was my New Year's resolution.

Taking a deep breath to calm my temper, I reply.

"I'm sure you would, but it's still a no. Please, help yourself to as much food as you want. My driver will take you home. Have a pleasant night." With that, I pivot out of my seat and quickly stride away from the table. On my way outside, I text my driver to tell him to take her home. I decide to walk to my mom and aunt's store. The fresh air will help me calm down. Electra better have a good explanation for whatever that was.

I walk inside the store, and before I have a chance to yell for my sister so I can ask her what the fuck she was thinking, I spot the most glorious woman I've ever seen. She twirls around, moving from behind a rack of clothes, letting out a spirited giggle. All I can think about is how much I want for her to spin her way into my arms.

"Just in time. I'm on my last sip." She drinks what's left in her glass and walks into the light, causing her amber locks to shine with gingery highlights.

"Drinking on the job? Is that wise? Christ, are you even old enough?" She spits champagne in my face, and immediately looks horrified. I lick my lips clean, groaning as I swipe more from my face with my fingers, rubbing them over my lips, savoring the taste of the liquid that graced her pouty pink lips. They're provoking me to find out what they taste like. I feel the urge to claim her, to make her mine.

She nods timidly and avoids looking directly at me. "Oh, Bonjour, Monsieur. I am so terribly sorry." Her milky skin flushes as she briefly raises her head to glance at me. When her eyes meet mine, my stomach lurches with desire. I fight the compulsion to rip off her clothes and explore how much of her body is affected by her pretty pink blush. "I'll go get a serviette or something."

She begins to turn, and I push down a strong urge to

grab her and make her stay. "It's more than fine and that won't be necessary." My words come out in a rush, sounding desperate. I can't bear to watch her walk away from me.

"Oh, well. I-I, umm... We are closed for the evening."

"Ah, I see. Even for say... the son of the owner?"

"Oh! Well, I-I'm sure that's fine... in that case."

"I'm Stefano by the way. And who are you, sweetness?"

"Stefano. Oh, um... hi, it's very nice to meet you." All I can hear is her lush exotic voice caressing the syllables of my name. It takes everything inside of me to fight off my impulse to her body against mine and worship her lips until they forget how to say anything else. The only thing that brings me back to reality is the need to know the name of the first woman to ever make me want to lay the world at her feet, who makes me want to indulge her every whim so long as she lets me keep her with me forever.

"I'm, Chloé De – uh, Marini. Chloé Marini." Chloé. The exotic Parisian name, spoken with her luscious accent, has just become my favorite sound in the world.

Her shyness is absolutely precious, and it leads me to think that she only allows a select few to see her for who she really is. For the true goddess that she is. I want to open her up so badly, to see her go wild for me. Only me.

"Chloé," I groan. I can't stop admiring her beauty. I can't think of anything to say. I'm completely frozen. My mind is blank. Between her striking smile and those entrancing jewel-like eyes of hers, I can't bring myself to look away. She's slowly rocking back and forth, her hands clasped behind her back. I can't stand that she feels so uneasy around me. Although it's hard to be upset about it. The way her nervous energy manifests is so damn cute. I bite back a chuckle.

"Oh my, is there something on my face?" She looks up at me with her beaming cerulean eyes, giving me the most dazzling smile. I can't believe it's real. I can't believe *she's* real.

I want to see that smile on her face as she walks down the aisle towards me, ready to become my wife. The unusual thought has me shaking my head and laughing at how crazy I've become, and how little I care about going insane. It feels right. Natural. Perfect. I never would have believed I could feel this way until I saw her. Every piece of my soul, all my most basic instincts, are saying one thing, and one thing only. Chloé Marini will be Chloé Montagne one day. One day very soon, if I have anything to say about it.

Her fingers stroke across her face as she checks to see if there is actually something on her face, finally snapping me out of my stupor. I force myself to say something before she starts to think I'm flat-out deranged. "Just the prettiest smile I've ever seen." I grin, only to get a confused frown in return. She puts her hands back behind her and a flash of light from her finger makes me feel like I've been sucked inside a pit of despair. My jaw clenches and I feel my molars begin to ache.

My mind is racing. I need to know if what I saw is the thing I fear most. "You're married?" I ask, my voice coming out strangled.

She nods, doing her best to avoid making eye contact with me.

"What's is the lucky guy's name?" I can barely hear myself speak over the sound of blood rushing in my ears. Knowing his name will only make this worse. Still, I need to know.

"Gilles...Gilles Marini." She whispers, as if it's a dirty secret... or maybe that's just the way I'm choosing to hear it.

My heart sinks as my mind races, desperately seeking a solution. All I know is that this this isn't over. Far from it.

"Right. One second, sweets," I hold up a finger and pull out my phone, dialing my lawyer. He gets paid a fat retainer to guarantee that he answers immediately anytime my family calls. He's never let me down, and he doesn't this time either.

"Good evening, William. Yes, I want to know how long it will take for you to get a divorce finalized? Very good. I'll call you with details later."

She laughs at me, her head tilted and one eyebrow raised, looking at me like I've completely lost touch with reality. Maybe it's time for me to show her just how serious I am.

"You don't think that... Why would you... I'm not going to get a divorce. I don't believe in it." She's adamant, but defensive. It seems like she's hiding something. Her words don't match her eyes. I could swear that her eyes are telling me that she feels what I'm feeling. She can't just come into my life, turn it upside down, and expect me to just give up. I'm a Montagne. And soon she will be too. I don't care what it takes to make it happen.

I grin slyly, watching her reaction to me. "You're not? Hmm... we'll see about that, sweets." I move to her quickly, maybe too quickly. Chloé steps back, looking at the door as though it can save her. I grab my little fox by her hips before placing a kiss on each one of her soft cheeks. I muster all my restraint to force myself to pull back, knowing I need to leave now or I'm going to rush this sweet girl into something she isn't quite ready for.

"Goodnight, sweetness. I'll see you tomorrow." I promise, leaning in to kiss her cheek one last time.

Chloé gasps. She must think I'm going for her lips this

time because she pulls away from me. "Stefano, you... can't."

"I know I can't. Not yet, anyway. But... I can still dream about you, can't I?" I wait for her to return my grin before turning and walking out the door. Even if her gorgeous smile was accompanied by an eye roll, she still smiled. That's a start.

26
THREE-CHLOÉ

I cannot let Stefano find out that I'm not married. He has the strangest effect on me. It's like he's pulling me in and I'm having the hardest time fighting his magnetism. Mostly because, deep down, I don't want to. That's why I decided to switch my purity ring to my ring finger. He is quite possibly the best-looking man I've ever seen. It's absurd. I'm worried he isn't going to give up on this infatuation he seems to have with me. What worries me even more is that I don't want him to.

I'm supposed to be at work in twenty minutes and I'm starving because I skipped breakfast to fuss over my appearance. I didn't want to admit to myself that I was doing it for Stefano. The denial ran deep, and when it occurred to me, I rinsed my face clean and brushed out my curls. Now my face shows my exhaustion and my hair looks like I slept in a barn. *Freedom, this is to maintain my freedom.* I just hope that I remember that when Stefano is around, instead of all my sense being wiped away after one of his ridiculously sexy smiles.

I'm running around the condo in a panicked craze. I

can't be late. I can't. *Dammit... Where did I put my purse? Where the hell is my phone?* I'm still fumbling around looking for my stuff when there's a loud knock on the door. *Why is it so hard to remember to put things back where they belong?* I'm in the middle of giving myself a lecture when I open the door to find Stefano, looking like a madman as he stares at me intently before frantically pushing his way inside.

Stefano scans the condo like he's looking for monsters or something. It's insane. I love it. "Are you okay? Tell me you're okay." He stares deep into my eyes with a level of concern I've only ever witnessed from my mother.

"Oui, I'm perfectly fine. I'm going to be late though, so I need to go."

"Chloé, don't you dare. Don't even think about it. Not until you tell me why you didn't answer your phone. Do you have any idea how worried I was?" He shouts, and the concern in his tone melts away my inhibitions and lights my desire for him on fire.

I should probably react with anger, or at least try to come off sarcastic. Anything except letting him see how turned on I am. "Stefano, please. Just take a chill pill or something. It must have died and I – well, I don't know where it is. I can't find my purse either." I halt, all my frenzied energy draining away and leaving me exhausted.

Why is fate such a nasty, horrible bitch at the worst times? Right in front of my eyes, there's Stefano, picking up my purse as if he just won a prize. Of course! I forgot I tossed it on the console table when I got back last night. All I could think about was hiding in my bed until I could figure out what to do about my feelings for him. Clearly, I haven't reflected on them long enough, and I'm already looking forward to retreating in my bed for further contemplation later this evening.

"Chin up, sweets." His calloused thumb and forefinger grip my chin, lifting my head up slightly. Little tingles spread throughout my body, touching every nerve-ending with a pulsing spark. It's impossible to ignore the intensity between us. "I told Mom I was going to take you out for the day so you could enjoy the city." *Come on denial, where are you when I need you?*

I take a quick breath as I look away from him as casually as possible. "I don't think that is a very good idea. I mean, I've only worked there for one day. There is a lot that I haven't learned yet and –" My hand is doing just as much talking as my mouth as I pace around, the evidence of my nerves showing without my approval.

"What's wrong, sweetness? Are you afraid to be alone with me?" He cocks his deliciously, charming...*stupid* handsome face at me, just to further provoke me. It works. I start to get angry, and I'm ready to respond with fury... until he winks at me, and I feel my knees weaken.

"No, I just think it would be unfair to the other employees." Oui! Oui! I am absolutely scared out of my mind to be alone with him. As I hold on to the wall, I begin thinking about how I can't be around all the ... *sex* he radiates. All. Day. Long. I'll break a leg, or worse, my heart. This simply cannot happen.

"My siblings and cousins will just have to deal. You and I are booked solid all day." I'm out of excuses, out of reasons, and I've completely lost hope of holding onto my sanity. I am in so deep.

"Well, maybe Electra can come. I'll just text her and see what she is up to." I'm grasping at straws here, and now Stefano is holding my purse hostage over his head. I turn red-hot as I jump, in a foolish attempt to retrieve it. Stefano holds it firmly with one hand as he puts the other on my lower back so softly, I wonder if I'm imagining things until I feel goosebumps break out over my body.

"She didn't tell you, huh?" He guides me out the door, taking my keys out of my purse to lock up for me. "Electra is visiting our sister Mia for the weekend."

I don't know why it kind of hurts that she didn't tell me. "Oh, that's nice."

Stefano gives me a warm smile that contains something I really hope isn't pity. "It was last minute, sweets. I'm sure she sent you a text."

"Well, maybe. But how would I know? My purse and phone have been kidnapped," I growl, before chuckling at how ridiculous this is. He should look silly holding onto my emerald green shoulder bag but somehow this macho stud is pulling it off, probably because of all that stubbornness and confidence he has in spades.

"I might be convinced to let it go.... for a price." He points to his lips and gives me a charming wink that turns me on so much, I feel my panties flood.

"Stefano." I roll my eyes at him, trying to conceal how badly I want to pay that toll.

We get into the garage, and I hear two beeps coming from an expensive looking red car after Stefano pushes a button on the key fob in his hand. We get closer and I see the BMW emblem just before Stefano opens the door for me.

"Red is my favorite color," he whispers gently, his lips grazing over the shell of my ear as he gently runs his hand through my hair. I'm unable to collect myself enough to respond before the engine revs and Stefano takes control of the vehicle. I'm so aroused by him, my legs can't press together tightly enough.

Stefano drives us to an eclectic looking restaurant called

the Papermoon Diner. I noticed the building before he pulled into the parking lot and fell in love with all the colors. It's painted in bright blues and yellows, with pretty much every color of the rainbow represented in the details. The first thing I see when I get out of the car is a teal cow with fuchsia spots, with a neon green alien riding on its back. I can't wait to see what the inside is like. So far, my favorite part is the hot pink elephant on the roof.

We walk inside the most whimsical place I've ever seen. The whole restaurant is full of funky little trinkets and ornaments that look like they were crafted by the creepy Sid guy from *Toy Story,* the kid who fused different toys together. Stefano leads me over to an empty table for four that has a reserved sign in the middle of it, and gestures for me to sit down before taking the seat right next to me. Of course. Now I'm going to have to sit here and fight off the euphoria that threatens to drown me, thanks to the smell of his stupid delicious cologne. Every peppery, citrusy basil note drives me closer to blissed out delirium.

I order the bacon and cheddar pancakes and Stefano orders the Bananas Foster French toast. His eyes are intent on mine, the words sounding provocative when he orders. As soon as his order comes, I immediately have food envy. Mine is incredibly delicious but it can't possibly compete with caramelized bananas covered in a heavenly cream cheese sauce. Without me having to say a word, Stefano splits our meals so that we both have half of each dish. It unsettles me a little bit how it seems like he can read my mind sometimes.

By the time we're done, I'm barely able to walk at a turtle's pace due to stuffing myself past the point of comfort, and I'm almost willing to take Stefano up on his offer to carry me to the car.

Stefano drives me to our next destination, and I let out a gasp of excitement when I see where he's taking me. We both channel our inner children the second we enter the Baltimore Zoo.

It's like we can't see everything fast enough. Stefano makes me laugh so much it hurts my stomach even more than all those carbs. We go into a dark cavern filled with snakes and spiders and all the other creepy crawly things that make your skin tingle, and that's when Stefano decides it would be a good idea to keep running his fingers in a tickling motion over my arms. I almost scream the first time he does it, convinced one of the bugs had managed to get on me.

Later, he picks me up over his head in front of the penguins, pretending I'm flying to taunt the poor flightless birds. As we pass the tigers and see the lions, he roars thunderously at them, and I giggle uncontrollably. It is just as sexy as it is hilarious to watch him challenge the king of the jungle. The way this man makes my hormones race has been driving me crazy all day.

Stefano keeps searching my face, like he's looking the clue he needs to crack me open and make me spill all my secrets. I find myself having to tell more lies to keep up with my original, and I know if I'm not careful, the truth is going to slip out of me at some point. How am I supposed to keep this up for the rest of the day? I'm going to need a missile-sized miracle, that's for sure.

As we're headed towards the exit, Stefano pops into the souvenir store and I follow him in. He goes straight towards the elephants and picks up a purple one, having learned today that it's my favorite color. I decide to return the favor and search for the perfect stuffed animal until I spot a red ruffed lemur. I laugh, thinking of Stella when I see it. Perfect.

He lets me take a funny photo of him with it so I can send it to his mom. She responds a few minutes later with a voice message full of insane laughter. She's right, her family is totally crazy, but I really do like their particular brand of crazy. I don't think I've laughed this hard or had this much fun since... well, ever.

We head back to the harbor and Stefano parks in front of a pirate ship. I can't stop staring at it, even after I hear my door open. Stefano reaches for my hand to help me out, just like he's been doing all day. It's very old fashioned and I didn't think I would like that kind of thing, but the way he does it makes me feel so cherished.

He leads me onto the ship, and I see a picnic spread out across a long wooden table. The crew members are all dressed as pirates, and they encourage us to join them by handing us leather hats that they call tricornes, before giving us each our own eye patch. We take a seat at the table and feast on delicious cheeses and antipastos while the pirate crew sails us around the bay.

I laugh at Stefano when he points to his eye patch while trying to keep a straight face. "Arrrrgh. Even with only one eye, I can still see that you're the treasure I've been searching for." His pirate accent is so bad, it's hilarious. *Does he think pirates are Irish?* It should sound like an extremely cheesy pickup line, heck, it does sound like a horribly cheesy pickup line. But it still makes my heart race with emotion. Who would have thought this mobster would be so goofy and loveable?

Oh, no. No. No. No. I'm pretty sure I am falling for him. What the hell am I going to do now? I wish I could just magically disappear to my bed for five minutes. Then I could face him again and not look at him like he's my whole world.

The sun is turning a golden orange hue as it lowers into

the horizon. It's very romantic, even with the crew member's ridiculous pirate-themed puns and jokes delivered without enthusiasm. I can imagine the whole pirate schtick would get old after doing it several times a day, every single day.

Stefano did bark out a laugh when our server joked about a pirate calling his mate on his 'aye phone.' But just as he went to tell us a joke about seeing a Jolly Roger rise, Stefano's face lost all trace of humor when he told him to stop there, or he'd make him walk the plank.

I don't know what Stefano's deal is, but he won't tell me the rest of the joke or why he got so upset about it. I know it's childish, but I decide to give him the cold shoulder until he agrees to tell me. I remain aloof for the rest of the day. I tell myself it's because I'm mad about him being so bullheaded, but really, I think I'm just trying to create some distance to avoid our sizzling chemistry.

Even though it didn't end well, today was one of the best days of my life. As soon as I make it back to the condo, I jump in the shower and climb into bed. After five minutes of trying to get comfortable, I huff out a sigh.

One second I'm freezing, the next it's hotter than hell in here.

Is this what love feels like? I *so* did not sign up for this. Suddenly I start sneezing and can't stop. I've counted five in a row when a dry cough scratches its way through my throat.

Great. My irrational feelings for the charming crime lord have made me so crazy that the lunacy is manifesting itself physically.

I allow myself a few minutes to be overdramatic before sending a text to Stella, telling her I'm not feeling well. She responds quickly, telling me she's on her way with medicine.

Stella arrives and instantly starts fussing over me. She insists I take the following day off as she stocks my fridge with soups and sorbets. Maybe having a sick day will give me some much-needed perspective. I sure as hell hope so, because I've never felt more lost than I do right now.

27
FOUR-STEFANO

My game plan is simple. Stone cold persistence. I am going to be the first and last person Chloé sees every day. That's not even part of the plan. That's just, well, it's because I just need to. That's all there is to it.

I got up extra early this morning after a mostly sleepless night, feeling unusually perky when I ordered a Chai tea and some chocolate pastries from our restaurant. I couldn't stop thinking about Chloé last night and how much fun we had. It was the best day. No, scratch that. The second best. The first was when I saw her for the first time. I can only think of a couple of things that could top that in the future. It won't be easy to top the euphoria I felt when we met.

Electra and Elias claim I've been cyberstalking her. I told them it isn't stalking because I'm just finding out everything I can about the future mother of my children.

That earned me a punch to the gut from my younger brother Roque. I was happy to return the favor, and we ended up wrestling for dominance before Máximo walked in and called out to Cruze and Ívan, who ran in to break us up.

That was a few minutes ago, and now I'm sitting around the table with my brothers, eating and laughing together. It's a pretty typical morning. Most of the time, Roque is getting into it with one of us. We all have a volatile temper, but he seems to have gotten the worst of it. One day very soon I'm going to use his hot-bloodedness to my advantage.

After breakfast, I continue my search and find way more than I bargained for. Not that I really had any idea what I was going to find. I was half expecting to see photos that would make me uncomfortable with the idea of other people having seen them, like pictures of her in a bikini or something. The last thing I expected to find was what looks to be some sort of photo journal. She posted one picture every day, each picture depicting more loneliness and desolation than the last. *Is this how my girl felt?* There isn't a single photograph of her.

I obsessed most of the night before, trying to think of ways to make her happy. I would do anything to see her incredible smile, but more importantly, I want her to have an incredible life, filled with everything she has ever wanted. If that means leaving her alone to be happy with her husband, then I will just have to live the rest of my life feeling gutted that the woman I love is out there with someone else.

I knock on Chloé's door with the tray of tea and treats. She opens the door and I stop thinking about how good it would feel to punch her husband in his stupid fucking face when I see how miserable she looks. I really am a prick. All I feel is joy that I get to be the one to take care of her. I guess I'm a selfish asshole after all.

"I'm sick...so," She starts to close the door on me, but I grab it firmly before it latches, pushing it open so I can slide past her and put the tray on the counter.

"*So*, that is why I'm here to take care of you." She gasps when I scoop her little body up in my arms and carry her into the bedroom. I take my time walking, relishing the sensation of having her body so close to mine, and before I'm ready to let her go, we are standing beside her bed.

I tuck her in gently, and as I'm placing a kiss on her forehead, I swear I see her fighting back a smile. "Stefano, you're going to get sick." My brain must be sick because I'm secretly wishing to catch whatever she has just so I can have her act as my sexy nurse.

"Don't worry about me, sweetheart," I assure as I enter her bathroom to inspect what my mom stocked it with. Just as I suspected, there are all kinds of medications in here. *What if she accidentally took this nighttime medication with an allergy pill? Nope. No way.* I start tossing away things that don't match any of her symptoms when I notice her standing at the door giving me the evil eye just as I toss her birth control pills into the wastebasket.

"Uh..." Her starry eyes drill into mine with so much heat I feel my forehead begin to perspire. "Do I really have to ask what you're doing?" I lift my shoulders nonchalantly as I measure out the correct amount of medication.

"Open," I guide the tiny measuring cup to her mouth, and she hesitantly opens up. "Good girl." I run my thumb over her lips, barely restraining the urge to kiss her.

Chloé sinks her teeth into my thumb hard enough for all the color to drain out of it. My cock goes rigid, and I dare her with my eyes to bite down even harder. She gasps and pushes me away. "Explain," she states firmly, but the two squeaky sneezes that immediately follow her command cancels out the authority in her tone. She sniffles and I hand her a tissue, but still her eyes are locked on me, demanding an explanation.

"What do you even need them for? You know, with your

husband being on active duty for the next four months and all?"

"Yeah. You're right. I um... just, you know, you never know. He could get temporary leave or something. It happens... all the time." I pick up the pills and begin to hand them to her, with every intention of handing them over. My fist doesn't get the message and furiously crushes the plastic with all my strength. I feel it cut into my skin, but I can't stop. Shit. I really can't stop.

Chloé is staring at me like I've lost my mind, and I think she's right. I need to get out of here before I confess that I'm hopelessly in love with a married woman.

"I-I'm so, so sorry. I don't fuck, I don't know what came over me." I can't stick around to see or hear her reaction right now. I'm barely handling mine as I rush out of the door. Once I'm in the elevator, I send my mom a text asking her to stay with Chloé. She agrees, so I'm shocked when she shows up at my door instead.

"Don't worry, Electra came back a day early for some reason, that she refuses to share with her dear mother. But I digress. She's checking on Chloé now."

"Thanks, Mom." It brings me some relief to know Chloé is being taken care of, but my mind is so wrecked, I don't think I'll be finding true solace anytime soon.

"What happened to my baby?" She asks me with a horrified expression as she inspects my hand.

"I've lost my mind. I'm a crazy person now."

"Come on, let's go upstairs so I can wrap that hand."

"Great, and after that you should probably commit me."

She searches my face, her eyes full of concern. "Stefano. What is this all about?" I don't know where to start but I know I need to talk to someone. Who better than the one person whose advice has never let me down?

My mom cleans and bandages my hand as I try to

explain all the madness going on in my life. "I can't be around Chloé anymore. I can't control myself around her. She's married and I can't do anything about it." I plop down on the couch and try to get comfortable. *This is where I live now. I'm never moving from this spot.*

"No way. Shit! She didn't tell me she was married." I look up to see Electra strolling into the room, holding a spoon in one hand and a container of yogurt in the other.

"Great... just great. I didn't know you were here. You were supposed to be with Chloé."

"She kicked me out. She didn't want to expose me to all her germs. Besides, don't you mean to 'thank you for letting me be in your presence, Queen Electra'?" She does a stupid little queen wave and I huff, rolling my eyes at her peskiness.

"Yeah, I am *so* thankful that I have such a brat for a sister. Lucky me."

"Watch it!" My father hollers at me from the other room. Seriously? Is the whole fucking family in the next room, listening to me talk about my unrequited love for Chloé?

"Untouchable!" Electra yells, raising her arms above her head and fluttering her fingers, fully embracing her role as the obnoxious little sister.

"So, who is this guy anyway? And should we track him down and make him disappear?"

"See, just when I start to think my life would be better without you as my sister, you bounce back into my good graces and I remember why I love you." I chuckle when she sticks her tongue out at me. "All I know is that his name is Gilles Marini and he's enlisted in the Air Force for the next four months. But who knows? He could come back at any point on leave."

Suddenly, Electra is holding her stomach and laughing

hysterically. What the fuck is so funny? I'm back to wishing she wasn't related to me. I feel myself scowling at her, and she finally calms herself down enough to speak. "No, no. I'm not laughing at what you think. He's an actor, bro. An actor. Look for yourself."

She types his name into her phone and hands it over. I scroll down, looking to see if he's married. He is, but his wife's name is Carole, not Chloé. I'm flooded with relief, and I feel joyful adrenaline rush through my veins. Nothing can stop me now. *Look out, Chloé. I will make you mine.*

28

FIVE-CHLOE

Stefano has been sending me mysterious gifts, the sweetest love notes attached to each one, for the past five days. I haven't seen him, haven't had the chance to forgive him in person because he had to leave for a business trip. It's probably for the best. I still don't know what I would even say to him. I can't claim to be angry at him, even though I know I should be. He did go all psycho on me while I was sick, but I can't forget the haunted look in his eyes before he ran out of my bathroom. More than his erratic behavior, that look is planted in my memory. So yeah, I've forgiven him. But I wish I could hold onto the anger. Everything would be so much easier if I could just hate him

I keep trying to forget how turned on I was by his display of jealousy and the fact that he was upset by me being on birth control. I can't help but wonder why he would care that I'm on the pill. All the possible answers have been driving me insane. But not nearly as insane as his little gifts.

The first day was a charm bracelet and a bouquet of my

favorite flowers, which are purple tulips. How on earth did he know that? The note read:

Soulmate

[sol-meyt] noun

Chloé, the person destiny has chosen for me, my missing piece, a connection of minds, and an unconditional, effortless, never-ending love.

Yours until the end of time,

Stefano

On the second day, more purple tulips came, along with a golden black-eyed Susan charm for my bracelet. The note is even more swoonworthy than the first.

Charismatic

Heavenly

Lovely

Opulent

Everything.

Yours until the end of time,

Stefano

The third day I got another charm. This one was a golden crab that really confused me, and the note didn't explain anything.

My sweet Chloé,

I am so in love with you. I miss you even though you're in my every thought. Even when I go to sleep, you are all I dream about. Still, I miss you every moment.

Yours until the end of time,

Stefano

The next day he sent me a charm of an orange and black bird that I'm not familiar with, which isn't all that surprising. I don't know much about birds. I'm really not a fan of them in general. Their chirping is the first thing I hear in the morning and being woken up by obnoxious sounds doesn't put me in the best mood. The attached note made me forget all about birds, though. All I could picture was Stefano doing things to me that I've never experienced before.

Sweetness,

My body is in agony being so far from you. The misery of picturing the things I would be doing to you right now but can't is too much for me. Kissing your delicious lips, deeply, lovingly... you are all I can think about. I need you close to me. Now and always.

Yours until the end of time,

Stefano

Today I received a golden charm in the shape of Maryland, along with another bouquet of tulips. The note was too short and left me aching for him.

Home is when I am holding you in my arms. I can't wait to be there.

Yours until the end of time,

Stefano

"You're reading them again?" Electra teases me for the zillionth time. "Oh, Chlo! You've got it so b-a-d." I wish she could step into my shoes for just a minute. It is so not easy being in love. She will understand one day. Especially when that person spontaneously leaves for five whole days, without even a proper goodbye.

"Excusez moi? That is not true. Not at all! I-I just... I don't understand why he didn't call or text to tell me goodbye, or why he left to begin with." She laughs even harder at my refusal to accept the truth.

"What? Your denial is hilarious, and your accent gets so thick when you're freaking out. You're adorable. No wonder my brother is obsessed with you."

"Happy to amuse you." I dramatically plop down on the overstuffed loveseat in the waiting room, letting out a huff of frustration.

"Okay, okay... I hate seeing you so miserable. I have it on good authority that he is coming home tonight." My eyes desperately search her face, wanting to be sure she isn't just teasing me before getting my hopes up.

"Really?" I squeal, sounding far too eager. I clench my mouth shut and wince as Electra fights backs a laugh. "Really?" This time I get it right, sounding way more reserved and far less desperate.

"Mom told me an hour ago that he was in the air."

"Are you sure? You aren't just teasing me, right?" There's really no reason to pretend to be cool at this point. She's been watching me pine over Stefano all week. I roll my eyes at myself. There's no sense in pretending I haven't fallen for him, either. I guess I'm beyond worrying about it. I am just so ready to see him again.

"I wouldn't play like that, girl! It's a surprise though, so you have to pretend you don't know. Capiche?"

"Yeah, yeah, yeah." I roll my eyes. "But I really need you to do me a solid. Please. I need to freshen up. I'm all sweaty and frizzy and who knows what else. I will close the store if you cover for me. Heck, I'll close for the rest of the week. I just need an hour or two."

"Deal," she agrees with a grin, and that's all I need to hear to get my butt in motion.

"You're the best," I shout on my way out of the door.

An hour later, I am out of the shower and applying my satsuma body oil, before getting into a sleeveless bright green bodycon dress that ends at my knees. I have on black high heels with red lips, curled hair, and my charm bracelet. I make it back to the store in just over an hour and Electra gasps when she sees me.

"Damn, girl! Lookin' good."

I roll my eyes at her and shoo her out the door. As soon

as she's gone, I start pacing impatiently. When is he going to get here?

I finally close up and head back to my condo. As soon as I get inside, I position myself at the window so I can see the cars that pull up. Every time I see one stop in front of the building, I get excited, only to be let down when someone other than Stefano steps out. I am filled with self-loathing. I hate feeling like a desperate, lovesick teenager.

I force myself to go sit on the couch, accepting that Electra was either misinformed or messing with me. My feet are killing me from wearing those stupid shoes for the last few hours. I could really use a...Wait did the tub just read my mind? I register the sound of water running from my bathroom. I know the facilities here are state of the art, but they don't just turn on by themselves.

I'm even more confused when I get to the bathroom and find the room dark. I flip the lights on, and gasp when I see Stefano leaning across the tub, shirtless. There are abs everywhere, and the words Soul Inside are tatted across his chest. He's wearing grey boxer briefs and I have to swallow the drool filling my mouth, wanting to maintain my dignity.

"Stefano...you're here."

"I am, and I know your secret, sweetness." The energy he's radiating is lethal, tempting me to climb his body and claim it for myself. "You're in big, *big*, trouble." Uh-oh. I should be terrified, but I find myself squirming, wanting more.

29
SIX-STEFANO

My little fox is in a world of trouble. With the light on, I can see her lush mouth coated in crimson and I bite back a groan. Her sultry lips are so divine, it is bittersweet torture to restrain myself from tasting them.

I'm going to break apart any moment now and devour her. "Sweets... next time you tempt me with those lips painted, I'm going to be thrusting my cock between them." She opens her mouth, only to snap it shut again. Her eyes fall to my erection, and she gasps as she watches me grab it and squeeze.

I stalk over to her and pick her up, swiftly moving towards the wall as I maneuver her legs around my waste. "Stefano, don't... please." I look at her small hands that are planted on my chest, wondering if she can feel my heart pounding for her.

"Don't what, sweets? Show you how much I love you, how good I can make you feel? Or show you how I'll keep that sexy smile on your gorgeous face all the time once you are mine."

Chloé eyes tear up as she presses her hands against my

chest, attempting to get out of my hold. "I can't be in this life. I can't! Not even if – "

"Not even if I gave it all up? I don't want it. I want you, Chloé. I love you."

"Oh, Stefano! I love you too. I missed you so much… and I hate you for leaving." She tries to glare, but her eyes are full of curiosity, giving her away. Huffs out from her winded speech with wide-open eyes full of curiosity. "Why did you leave?"

"I went to Italy."

"Without me?"

"Sweetness." I kiss the side of her lip, peppering a few more along her cheek. "I went to get permission to step down and have Roque take over. Then I went to France to get permission from your parents to marry you."

"And did they say all say yes?"

"The Godfather did. Don't worry, your parents will come around. In the meantime, they have a nice condo upstairs."

"Stefano, you… you didn't? You did? You kidnapped my parents?" Chloé can't seem to decide if she should laugh or be upset.

"Technically… I merely ordered it."

She rolls her gorgeous eyes at me. "Oh, I know how much you like to order things," she purrs, running a finger down my chest and getting my shaft riled up again.

"Hmm, sweetness. I do. But tonight, I'm going to let you lead."

"Does that mean I can do anything I want?"

"Yes, God, yes. Please. I can't wait to see you out of that dress. Seeing you bare for me is going to be a vision I will never forget."

"You first," she whispers nervously.

"You don't need to be shy with me baby." I take her

hand in mine, lifting it to my lips for a kiss before pressing it against my erection. "Go ahead, take them off for me baby." She pushes my boxer briefs down, looking shocked when they hit the ground and she witnesses all ten inches of my arousal standing at attention for her.

"It feels so strong and —"

Her small hand tightens as she slides it up and down my length.

"Oh, Chloé. That feels...mmm so good." I grab her hand, slowing her down when she picks up speed. I'm not ready to let go. Not yet.

"Your turn, sweets." She takes off her dress, leaving her in just a set of mint green lingerie embellished with frail lace. The expensive material would be so easy to tear off her luscious body.

"Dear lord. You are breathtaking." I give into my urge and rip her bra away from her breasts, feasting my eyes on perfection. She is exquisite. She looks so virtuous, so wholesome, so... pink. I want to corrupt her. I want to mark her, claim her.

"You are so sweet, so pure. So soft and delicate...so precious and shy, filled with so much innocence. God, I hate myself, Chloé. I'm going to take it all." I kiss her with abandon, her soft lips eating away at my self-control.

"Stefano, I want to so badly but... I don't know how. I mean I know *how*, but... I haven't you know... before."

"Oh, sweets. There isn't anything you need to know. I want you just as you are. This is the first time this will mean anything to me, and it means everything. It's going to be new for both of us. We can take it slow, any way you want to. No matter what, it will be perfect."

"I like the sound of that," she whispers.

I kiss her lovingly, holding her gently in my arms and showing her how much I cherish and worship her.

I feel her shiver and run my hands over her arms a few times. "Come on sweets, you're getting chilly, let's get in the tub." I help Chloé into the bubble bath scented with her orange blossom bubble bath before climbing in with her. We sit across from each other, smiling softly at one another. I stretch out, pulling my girl over my chest and kissing her tenderly. Soft kisses turn passionate and I never want to pull my lips from hers. I never knew a kiss could be like this. It's the kind that makes you think, *I could die right now, and I'd die the happiest man alive.* It makes everything in my life feel suddenly perfect. Like every choice I've made up until now was right because everything I've done has led me here, to this moment with Chloé.

We get lost in one another, and I only come out of the spell we've created when I realize that the water temperature has dropped significantly.

I drain some of the water out and add in more bubble bath and enough hot water to make it comfortable again.

Chloé straddles my hips, running her slickness over my erection, truly challenging my ability to hold myself in check. "If you want me inside of you, you're going to have to make it happen," I grumble hoarsely, trying to maintain my composure with every breath I take.

"Stefano, I do." She takes a deep breath, stroking my length between her folds. I feel her minty exhale against my cheek as she uses her tiny hand to slowly guide me into her virgin pussy. "I want you so much." She grips the rest of my girth, so hard I start to see stars. That or she's sparkling. She has never looked more ethereal.

"I do too, sweetness," I tell her lovingly, and as I break through the barrier of her virginity, I put my ring on her finger. Chloé moans, smiling at me before bringing her sweet lips to mine. When she finally pulls away, I promise, "We can make it official tomorrow."

She begins moving on top of me, but she suddenly stops, whimpering, "Stefano, it hurts. There's so much pressure." My girl tries to get comfortable as her body adjusts to a ten-inch foreign object. I can tell she's just as eager as I am, but we have our whole lives and I need her to be able to walk down the aisle tomorrow.

"Relax for me, baby. Rest your head on my chest and let our bodies get used to each other for a little while." She gives me a warm smile before laying her upper body against mine and nuzzling my neck with her lips.

"It will feel good soon, so good," I promise as I palm her bottom, roughly squeezing the flesh.

"I like this. It's...mmm, cozy. Mmm. Stefano, that. Oh, I like that too." I move my hand over her cunt, fisting it in my hand greedily before tracing circles around her clit.

"I love making you feel good. You look so beautiful like this." I press my fingers harder, digging them into her flesh deeper and receiving the hottest murmurs in response.

"More of that, oh, please." Fuck me, I love hearing her begging for me. Seeing how much she needs me. It's the best damn feeling in the world.

"Oh, baby. I'm going to give you more. So much more. Sweetness, we're starting our family tonight. Right here." I cup her breasts in my palms, massaging them as my thumbs flick over her pebbled nipples. She jerks when I wrap my mouth around her breast, drawing my tongue around her areola in between flicks and devouring suction.

"I-oh, Stefano, oui, oui, oh. Oh, ahh, I'm – mmm." As amazing as her orgasm feels, I'm captured by the way her face lights up as she giggles through her moans during her climax. It is beyond breathtaking. She is beyond breathtaking.

"Oh, sweets... Sweets, you're taking my seed so well," I groan as I fill her up.

"It's...mmm, it's so warm." She bites her lipstick-stained pout, tempting me to kiss her until her lips are good and swollen.

"Sweetness, I am going to keep you filled with my warmth all night long." I put her delicate hand in mine, positioning it over my rapidly rising erection. I've been fantasizing about her for give days and now I have her all alone. All to myself. For the whole night. And... it is my turn.

30
EPILOGUE-CHLOÉ

"Come on, baby... Just think, you can tell your little friends that you slept with a celebrity."

"Ew, no! And like I said before, I'm married." This egotistical A-lister is a hard-headed snob and a half. He's also super hyper and he clearly forgot to rub in the powder on his nose. Or his make-up artist forgot. Either way, it's very noticeable.

I look around as I smell my favorite scent. I feel my heart racing as the hairs on my neck lift from the sensation of Stefano's heated breath growling over my skin.

"To this stud?" Hollywood's flavor of the month gushes with enthusiasm as he looks Stefano up and down. "Do you swing?" His brow curves with hopeful interest.

"From time to time." Stefano provokes him with a devilishly handsome smile. Sometimes this side of him needs to be indulged and there isn't always a bedroom or a private corner to be had. His wild side needs release, and it really turns me on.

"Re-ally?"

"Yeah, really!" Stefano grins as he punches him,

crushing the famous piece of trash to the floor. He gets up, stumbling as everyone watches him and laughs.

He waves his hands around making eyes at the crowd, but he doesn't make eye contact with anyone in particular. His bleeding lip kicks up into a goofy smirk. "I'm okay. Totally fine. Slipped, you know how it is?" Everyone looks away when he turns around, walking strangely and holding onto his lower back.

"Better?"

"Not really. He got off easy. I'm the calm one in my family."

"The calm one?" I can't help but chuckle at the fact that although he is far from calm, his statement is true. "When did that happen?" Still, it is so entertaining to provoke my husband. The rewards are often orgasmic.

Stefano swats my bottom before giving it a possessive squeeze. "Hilarious, sweetness, hilarious. Have we stayed long enough yet?"

"Stefano, it's our baby shower." I'm annoyed by the social obligation too, but a commitment is just that. I used to crave having a life like just this, filled with parties and friends. But I know better now. Life is better surrounded by the people you love, people you call family. Even if that family is totally insane.

Stefano comically rolls his eyes at me, giving me that charming smirk I adore so much. "No, it isn't. Our real baby shower will be with our family. This is just a weird circus event orchestrated by a client who doesn't understand boundaries."

"Come on! You know Scarlett has been a great friend to me." He huffs and shrugs his shoulders, trying to be agreeable even though I know he isn't going to join my new friend's fan club anytime soon.

I look down and notice Stefano's knuckles are red and

scraped. He isn't showing any pain but it could swell or get infected. "Let's get that cleaned up then we can make our excuses."

"Mmm, is it really an excuse? I would just rather be at home having my wife's tightness wrapped around my fat cock all night."

My face flushes and so does my sex. I haven't had dry underwear since the day I met him. I keep spares in my purse, but strangely they seem to disappear frequently. "Stefano, we're in public, you can't!"

"Oh, I beg to differ. You're mine now, sweetness. Mine to do with whatever I want." Oh, I can't wait to find out what that is. Stefano never fails to deliver on his sexy surprises.

"I'll consider it, Mr. Montagne...on two conditions. First, we say goodbye like respectable human beings... Then I want you to take me home and do that animalistic thing you do with your tongue."

"Your wish is my command, Mrs. Montagne." I giggle when he scoops me up in his arms. "For the record, I don't trust her. And I have our new security guy Axel looking into her."

"Always so protective." I whisper in his ear seductively. It turns me on so much when he gets like this. Ever since we found out I was pregnant, he's been even more attentive. We are rarely apart, which some might find strange, but the thing they don't understand is that Stefano and I are better together. As a team. I'm never lonely anymore. That feeling of isolation is nothing but a faint memory. Stefano and I both feel so lucky that we get to spend every single day with our favorite person. People can call us any evil name they want. It can't hurt us because we know the truth. Although, Stefano is quite the dirty devil when he's turned on. Which is most of the time. Hmmm... Maybe he is the spawn of Satan. I think I'll keep him anyway.

Stefano holds me tighter to his chest. "You love it." I moan with approval, feeling right at home in my husband's strong arms. I don't want him to ever let go.

Stefano would do anything for me. I love him so much. "Je t' aime." And I would move mountains for him. There is nothing I wouldn't do to make him feel the way he makes me feel. "Je t' aime."

"I love you too, sweetness. And hearing you say it makes me so damn hard. Let's make our excuses quick, before this monster takes over." Oooh. We really should hurry. He is an absolute madman when his monster gets free. I love it.

ABOUT THE AUTHOR

Alana Winter's passion for creating stories and characters has always fueled her active imagination. She graduated from Valencia Film School with a degree in film technology. There she dabbled with screenplays without much success. It took a while to find her niche which ended up being what she loved reading the whole time. Now she spends her time creating witty, suspenseful and sexy characters that go on a wild journey together. The men she writes about aren't always heroes but they're always passionate, provocative and possessive.

I love hearing from readers through reviews and social media. Feel free to reach out to me anytime.It's so helpful and motivational to me. Thank you so much for supporting indie authors!

*Would you like access to exclusive sneak previews that aren't around anywhere else? What about new releases, Easter eggs, deals and promotions or freebies from other InstaLove authors?

Sign up to get my Newsletter here.

ALSO BY ALANA WINTERS

Age-Gap Romances:

Killian: A Boyfriend's Older Brother Age Gap Romance

Braxton: A Football Romance

The Baker's Peony: A Age-Gap Romance

Homegrown Hero: A Fire Marshal/Artist Romance

Military Romances:

Yule Be Mine: A Holliday Military Romance

Commanding Her Heart: A Age-Gap Military Romance

Lucky Star: A Cowboy Romance

Mafia Romances:

Vanished In Baltimore: A Captive Mafia Romance

Amour Noir: A Mafia Romance

Forbidden Muse: A Rockstar Mafia Romance

Dark Romances:

Throne Of Lies: A Dark Mafia Romance

Steplover: A Taboo Romance Thriller

Forever Lover: Sequel To Steplover

Fantasy Romances:

A Touch Of Envy: A Royal Captive Fantasy Romance

Silent Night Stalkers: A Reverse Harem Vampire Fantasy Romance

Finders keepers…sorry bro that's not how things are going to go.

Isabella:

My mother died unexpectedly and without her I feel lost and numb.

I'm an orphan now and I have to move in with my estranged grandmother.

I meet the sweetest guy next door and before I know it we are dating.

He's so good to me and good for me.

So, why is it that I can only think about his gorgeous older brother that somehow makes me feel alive again?

Killian:

I'm a professional boxer or I was until my knee went out on me and it was the last injury my body could handle.

I moved back to the home I grew up in to watch my brother and my fathers company.

My life feels bland and monotonous.

Then I meet Bella.

My dream girl. My obsession. My brother's girlfriend.

I'm powerless under her spell.

She brings color back into my life.

I know we were meant for each other.

She is mine and I'll move heaven and hell to bond her to me forever.

Excerpt:

"My brother is just a boy. You need a man! You need me and you know how much I need you cuore mio, mia Bella." (My love, my beauty.)

Warning: This insta-love story is a suspenseful romance with a HEA. Some of the dark themes in the story include drug use, abuse, graphic violence and descriptive sexual scenarios that may be triggering. Please read with caution and discretion.

I found a real Goddess today and I'm going to go the whole nine yards to keep her in my life.

BRAXTON:

I've been called Italian stallion, gunslinger, MVP, jock and sidow.

That last one is a combo of sibling and widow.

It was given to me by the media two years ago, after my brother died.

Losing Sterling broke me.

I feel as if I'm only working to stay alive. Not that I feel alive.

That's until I get blindsided by a precious woman cheering in the stands and everything in me cheers back.

Simone is a game changer, but she thinks I'm a player.

I'll show her that the only thing I'm playing for is keeps.

Nothing will stop me from tackling her heart.

SIMONE:

I've been called cookie, hot cakes, sugar bomb, cupcake and spice girl.

You hear it all when you work at a bakery.

I love baking, but I do not love being looked at like I'm on the menu.

Although, it's not so bad when it's coming from Braxton.

The man is a certified stud muffin with the best pound cake I've ever seen.

I know better, you can't have your cake and eat it too.

I'd have to be half baked to think that I won't get burned if I give him a chance.

He won't yield and keeps bringing my body to a rolling boil

You know what they say, if you can't stand the heat, get out of the kitchen.

Possessive QB is a standalone romance with a HEA, no cheating and no cliffhanger.

Every Woman In The World Wants Iverson Vogel.

Iverson:

The cover of a magazine labeled me the hottest man alive.

It ruined dating for me.

I don't have time for it anyway.

I'm a celebrity chef that has been running several bakeries.

I've recently sold them, ready for a new start.

I'll be signing the papers to make it official at a home-cooked meal with the new owner.

When I meet his daughter, all I can think about is owning her. Then taking her straight to the courthouse to make it official.

Peony:

I've never wanted someone more than I want Iverson Vogel.

His passion for baking inspires me to create and try new recipes.

He's also extremely famous, ridiculously good-looking, and spectacularly talented.

I know he is way out of my league.

Too bad my heart isn't getting the message.

I'm sure meeting him in person will simmer my silly infatuation.

Or will it boil out of control?

A Possessive Daddy Insta-Obsessed Romance so hot it could fry an egg. No cheating and a swoony HEA.

My Best Friend Already Feels Like My Brother...I Think This Christmas, I'll Make It Official.

I'm a Marine on a new mission.

One that will require me to use everything I've got in my arsenal.

My best friend is taking me back home with him for the holidays.

This seems like a bad idea right away.

I'm a workaholic who is more comfortable being alone.

I thought I was settled and happy enough.

Meeting Eric's sister changed everything and my everything just became about her.

Now all I want for Christmas is to find a way to earn Natasha's heart.

This holiday insta-love story is safe and it ends with a sweet HEA.

*Cortez saves her when she **needs** it the most. Finding Emmy is what he **needed** the most.*

Emmy's new boss is too perfect.

He's a handsome, older man who enjoys tempting her. She's fighting falling for him.

The temptation is unbearable.

Cortez makes her heart feel it's bursting.

He gives her body goosebumps.

He puts her brain on overload.

He's trying to break down her walls.

She can't let that happen.

Cortez is a Navy Veteran.

He's been raising his son on his own since he was six months old.

When Miles starts going to school, he feels lost.

That is until he meets a beautiful bombshell who takes his breath away.

Suddenly, he's making plans to expand his family.

He wants everything from Emmy.

Her laughter, her body, and *command* of her heart.

They're both wounded. Can they heal each other? Or will, they bring each other down?

I'm a realist.

Never believed much in superstitions or luck.

That all changed when I came home to my ranch and met our new hire.

Now, I feel like a lucky son of a gun, wishing for this little Star to be all mine.

I've always liked to play with fire. Now it's playing with me. Stella has kindled my dark heart, ignited my desires and set my world ablaze.

Before my life could even begin, it almost went up in flames.

Smoke alarms saved our lives.

The sound put my mother into labor.

The fire forged a powerful force in me.

I find resolve in its embers.

My enemies find themselves scorched by it.

It has never consumed me...not until I met its infernal match —Stella.

The red-hot firestorm that has me burning for more.

Chloé:

I'm a long way from home. Thankfully my life in France is behind me. Being a Mafia princess has brought me nothing but misery. The paparazzi in the states don't even care who I am. Unlike Stefano who wants to know everything. I can't let him find out who I really am or about my other secret. It will ruin everything.

Stefano:

I'm headed to Amour Noir to get an explanation from my sister, Electra. It better be good, too. I would have rather swam with sharks tonight then gone on that date she just set me up on. I'm all fury when I walk in, wincing my eyes to when I see the sweetest little thing twirling my way. I step into the light, scaring her into spraying the sip of champagne she took in my face. Her fear turns to shock when my tongue cleans the alcohol dragging it slowly as I wonder what my future wife's lips taste like.

I'm singing my biggest hit for the billionth time when my gaze meets a pair of rich hazel eyes that shine brighter than the most precious metal.

The romantic lyrics of my song feel truly meaningful for the very first time.

My heart and soul begin pouring out of me through every word.

This seductress is way too young, too tempting, and too precious to be starring in my filthiest fantasies.

It doesn't matter though; she became mine the second she flashed her flirtatious smile at me.

That smile is driving me to act on my most basic urges.

I refuse to let anyone or anything hold me back.

My passionate serenade turns into a heated, seductive performance.

It's just the two of us lost in this euphoric trance.

Then, within the blink of an eye, she is taken away from me.

My soul was soaring in her presence, but in her absence, it is crashing to the ground, shattering into a million pieces.

Her father is a ruthless, powerful man who will stop at nothing to keep her from me. But he's in for a rude awakening.

He's about to learn that not even a Mafia King can stop a Rock-and-Roll God when he's found his eternal muse.

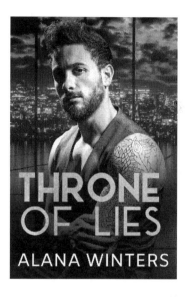

Ready or not... you're mine.

Javier Vidal:

I'm working toward bringing the most influential man in the nation's capital down. My father has monopolized the media industry, which veils my uncle's covert Mafia empire. Using a formidable divide-and-conquer strategy put the fate of the economic and political elite in my father's hands. It's imperative I take control of things before it's too late. My life is full of secrets, but the one I must protect at all costs is my obsession. Aveline

Bianchi. She is now in my web. Trapped by a ruthless, territorial criminal mastermind. The demons inside me bring my most carnal impulses to the surface, pushing me to dominate her. To break and defile her. I must fully possess her—body and soul.

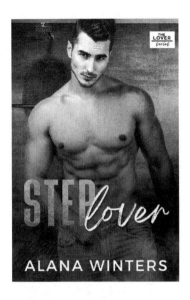

You're not supposed to fantasize about your stepsister.

You're not supposed to desire having everything with her.

Our love is forbidden, where all I can hope for are stolen dark nights.

When it comes to Skyler, I'm grateful for whatever I can get...for now.

Nothing will stop me from claiming and loving her for the rest of my life.

An erotic romance series with a twist, and an alpha male lead that knows what he wants and won't stop until he gets it.

Warning: This story is intended for adult readers. It contains some dark themes that may be triggering for some readers.

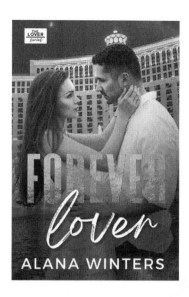

Jasper:

My family didn't go into hiding because I married my stepsister as many assume.

No, we got out of dodge and moved to Nevada after getting one short, life altering text from Carver.

Everything could be paradise in our new lives here, if paranoia didn't haunt us.

I've done everything in my power to keep my loved ones safe.

Carver will be making a huge mistake if he comes for us again… because I'll be ready this time.

Carver:

Last year didn't work out so well for me.

This year, I'm fully prepared to take care of my unfinished business.

I've even taken drastic measures to avoid being recognized while I find myself on an adventurous cross country road trip.

Staying under the radar seems impossible when I meet a sexy, spitfire who can't be ignored.

This enigmatic woman demands attention, and she has all of mine.

The sequel to Steplover is a dark, spicy romance with voyeurism, anti-heroes, and exhibitionism with a HEA. It's suited for ages 18+

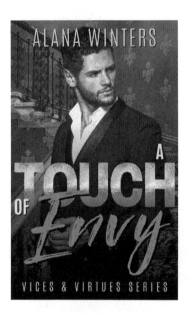

Truly. Madly. Deeply—Obsessed.

Once Upon A Time...

Princess Aiya was tired of playing the role of the perfect princess.

She was always sure to say and do all the right things.

Her new life with Prince Adirion would surely be the same.

The only choice she had was to accept her future.

Until a man shrouded in mystery and temptation gave her a way out.

King Slaine ruled the most feared kingdom.

A conqueror fixated on taking Prince Adirion's bride-to-be.

Driven by a love so pure...so timeless—it's fantastical.

Fueled by *envy,* King Slaine spurred a brutal rebellion that had devastating consequences.

Will capturing the princess ruin his chances of getting her to fall for him?

A Royal Captive Romance with a possessive anti-hero who is insta-obsessed with the object of his affection.

The Future's Fate Lies In Three Mates.

On a nightly stroll, I rest upon a tree only to find myself in a strange place and time.

A dark mysterious man, finds me.

I think I'm saved until I realize I'm being held captive by three wildly possessive men.

They won't let me go until I've completed a strange ritual meant to save the world.

Is it destiny? Or is it a trap?

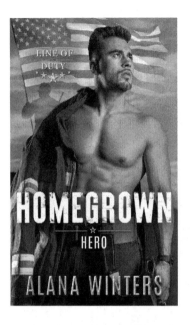

Their Fire Is Too Explosive To Be Put Out.

KAI MAHINA

Fighting fires is in my blood.

For four generations, my family has worked at the same fire station.

I live a simple life in a small town where nothing ever changes.

That is, until a movie studio decides to film here.

My Chief gives me the opportunity to work on their set.

The first day completely changed my life.

In one look, I know I found the girl of my dreams.

Her boss is trying to keep us apart, wanting her for himself.

When an electrical fire breaks out, I spring into action.

I'm thrust into the spotlight for saving the crew and the movie star.

The unwanted attention drives a wedge between Micaela and me.

But that just drives me to work even harder to prove that, despite our age gap and differences, I'm the man for her.

No matter what it takes, I will be claiming Micaela as all mine.

Warning: Kai is an OTT Possessive male who mildly stalks his love to get to know her better.

Made in the USA
Columbia, SC
08 August 2024